RIO GRANDE SHOOT-OUT

Situated on the Rio Grande at the southernmost tip of Texas, Brownsville was a nowhere place hundreds of miles from the bloody conflict between the states. Consequently, the town was having a quiet war, with ordinary folk just trying to make a living. But throw in soldiers, renegades and undercover agents, with a heavy dose of hatred and vengeance, and the mix can only lead to violence — and a shoot-out on the Rio Grande.

D1456539

Books by Ethan Wall
in the Linford Western Library:

HIGH PLAINS DEATH

ETHAN WALL

RIO GRANDE SHOOT-OUT

Complete and Unabridged

LINFORD
Leicester

First published in Great Britain in 2004 by
Robert Hale Limited
London

First Linford Edition
published 2005
by arrangement with
Robert Hale Limited
London

British Library CIP Data

Wall, Ethan
  Rio Grande shoot-out.—Large print ed.—
  Linford western library
  1. Western stories
  2. Large type books
  I. Title
  823.9'14 [F]

  ISBN 1–84395–616–0

Published by
F. A. Thorpe (Publishing)
Anstey, Leicestershire

Set by Words & Graphics Ltd.
Anstey, Leicestershire
Printed and bound in Great Britain by
T. J. International Ltd., Padstow, Cornwall

This book is printed on acid-free paper

To Stella, for believing in the manuscript during its difficult early stages.
And to Lance for . . . well, for just being Lance.

1

'Fire!' Captain Stewart bellowed.

Gunfire exploded around him and, ahead, Confederate soldiers began to fall.

'We've got 'em on the run, sir!' his lieutenant shouted.

'Advance!' Stewart yelled.

On the order, the line of blue pushed on, forcing the Confederates back. The lieutenant repeatedly pulled the trigger of his Colt, his arm extended ramrod straight, each of his shots bloodying a target.

The unit had been advancing towards the Corinth Road when they'd run into a small Southern group near a dense oak thicket known by locals as the Hornet's Nest. There had been an exchange of fire during which the enemy had been pushed back to entrench themselves near the thicket.

After a lull, there were signs the Southerners were preparing to retreat in recognition of the superior numbers of Union men. It was then the captain had given his order.

The young lieutenant relished action, quickly reloading and pumping more lead at the grey-uniformed figures.

It is historians who put names on battles and neatly map out encounters putting logic on events. But in the thick of the fighting there is no neatness. At the time, the generals in their headquarters might have some idea of strategy, but for the men on the ground it is mayhem and confusion.

And so it was for Lieutenant Newland. History was later to label the present carnage as the Battle of Shiloh. For him it was a mess of blood and bullets. But it was also an opportunity. Ever since guns had startled crackling in the grey light of dawn he had been looking for his chance. It might come that day, it might come later. He was a patient man.

Unrelentingly the Federals progressed, up to the oak thicket and beyond. Eventually, still under the continuous barrage of bullets and shot, the Confederates made it to a distant screen of trees. An extensive open patch now separated the two groups of combatants.

'Cease fire and entrench,' the captain ordered. The firing from the Union men became spasmodic then ceased as his men dropped to the ground, Confederate fire still continuing.

'We'll be sitting ducks trying to cross that open ground,' the captain said. 'We'll circle them. It's going to be difficult getting at them but that way, we can at least bottle them up while we await further orders. See that ridge on the left? You take a unit and pin them down from there.'

Crouching low, Newland ran along the line. He picked a dozen men and they made their way round the wood. Topping the ridge he stopped in his tracks. Jesus! There was a massive

Confederate force heading their way!

'Back!' he shouted to his men, gesturing with a wide sweep of his arm.

He was part way on his return when he saw a reconnaissance rider come round the thicket from the opposite direction and drop from his mount near the captain. He heard the yelled words: 'A whole reb brigade. Half a mile distant. Coming this way.'

'And that ain't all,' Newland said when he finally made the captain's side. He pointed back. 'Coming up on over the ridge. More of them. Must be brigade strength too.'

'Shit' the captain mouthed. 'Right and left. Now *we're* the ones being pincered. Nothing for it.' He pointed to the vast knot of oak trees. 'Get everyone into the thicket. It's large enough. We'll make a stand there.'

Once they'd made cover they found a major and other Federals already there, having been forced into the thicket by the unexpected arrival of Confederate reinforcements on the other side. The officers from the varied troops got together. Captain Stewart ordered Newland to stay with his unit and keep watch. Newland saluted and for a moment watched his commanding officer join the others.

He loathed the man. The fellow came from common farming stock as betrayed by his casual use of 'shit' and other cursing. No idea of the way to behave. On the other hand Newland was from an army family. A West Point graduate, he was a regular who didn't think that mere volunteers like Stewart should be granted commissions.

It galled him that such a farming hick — who'd only carried a uniform since news of the outbreak at Fort Sumter — should be above him, giving him orders.

What was worse, for a long time Newland had realized that he himself had hit his limit in the promotion ladder. He didn't know why. He played by the book, kept his boots shined. But others knew: under his spit and polish he was incompetent. But, like most with a severe failing, he couldn't see it. All he knew, he had borne a lieutenant's insignia for eighteen months, which was longer than Captain hay-prodding Stewart had been in the damn army!

Some distance away from him the officers continued their deliberations. They were all part of the invasion force which had come up the Tennessee River and occupied Pittsburg Landing. Their orders had been to seize the Memphis & Charleston Railroad to cut off the Confederates' link with the east coast. Their objective, Corinth, the Confederates' most important rail junction in the west, was now almost achieved, mere miles away. But now, with the massing Confederates around them, their target could have been the other side of the continent.

Each of the officers had his say but it all came to the same thing. Despite their own added numbers they knew they were going to be vastly overwhelmed by the Confederate additions. The major took their counsel, nodded in agreement and reluctantly gave the order to retreat.

The order was passed to the ranks and the men began to work their way back through the tangle of oaks. But by the time they were emerging into the clear, the enemy forces from both left and right were solidly in view. The sight of reinforcements gave the small unit in the far wood the confidence to break cover and make slow advance on the thicket.

Union blue once again visible, Confederate guns began to crackle, rising to a non-stop fusillade. The Federal men broke into a run, back-firing when they could. For the second time that day the same terrain of furrowed fields and grassland became a bloody battlefield.

The Union men worked their way back over a landscape defiled by dead and wounded men of both sides. The moans of already-downed men were interlaced with spasmodic screams as other unfortunates joined them on the blood-soaked earth. God knows the fate of those injured men still living . . . a bayonet from a passing soldier . . . a lonely, lingering death in the darkness of the Tennessee night . . .

Newland and the captain were at the back of the retreat firing their hand pistols at the advancing rebs. A half-hour later, such shots were tokens as, thankfully, the gap was widening — the Union men were running while the Confederates were satisfied with a slow but unrelenting walking pace. Similarly rebel bullets too were finding fewer targets.

When the gap had become around two hundred yards the leg-weary captain and lieutenant fell to a walk, satisfied to retreat and return occasional fire.

'I don't see Grant having enough manpower to stop this lot,' Stewart shouted. He was some yards behind the lieutenant. 'It's Bull Run all over again.

We're in the shit again. Either a Confederate bullet or drowning when the bastards push us into the river. Ain't gonna be time to organize a safe river crossing this time.'

Ramming new rounds into his pistol Newland glanced back as the captain spoke. But, walking backwards, he didn't see a shallow dip in the ground behind him and he fell backwards. He scrambled to one knee, making to get up. In doing so, he looked around. It was mayhem. Their own soldiers were now way back, shouting, running. Yet, now and again, one of them would manage to reload and throw a little lead back at the advancing Confederates.

Stewart drew level with Newland and looked down into the indentation. He extended a hand to help his comrade out. But the lieutenant dropped back into the hollow. Having assured himself that he was unseen by others, he raised his reloaded gun and pulled the trigger. The bullet caught Stewart in the shoulder. He spun round and pitched into the dip beside him. The lieutenant ignored the widened, puzzled eyes, slammed his barrel against the man's temple and fired.

With a feeling of satisfaction, he leapt up and loped after his men.

★   ★   ★

By dusk the Federal survivors were back at Pittsburg Landing, licking their wounds. The Union had not achieved a major victory since the beginning of the conflict. Their only compensation in the present defeat: news had filtered through the lines that General Johnston, the Confederate leader, had been killed by a stray bullet.

In addition to the general, there were over ten thousand men dead, wounded or missing.

And there was one among that number who had not been killed by something coming out of an enemy barrel.

★ ★ ★

In a tent surrounded by bedraggled, snoring comrades-in-arms, Newland dropped onto the bed. The coarse-mannered farm-boy wearing a captain's pips and now sprawled out on the battlefield had been wrong. They hadn't been pushed into the river. At nightfall the Confederates had halted their advance short of Pittsburg Landing and bivouacked in preparation for the final assault in the morning.

Even if they had continued through the darkness they would not have found the operation to be the pushover they were expecting. During the initial routing of the Union forces two more divisions had crossed the river, providing an extra twenty thousand men for the next day's encounter.

Now, Newland mused, if there is going to be a pushover, it is going to be the other way.

And with that happy thought he was soon asleep.

* * *

He was nudged awake by a corporal on General Grant's staff.

'You have been summoned to the general's quarters, sir.'

Newland rubbed his face and got to his feet. 'Lead the way, corporal.' He brushed his hands down his uniform and followed the soldier to the general's tent.

The general was standing at a table poring over maps with his subordinate officers and newly arrived generals. Newland stood quietly at ramrod attention. Eventually the general looked up. Newland stiffened even more and saluted. 'Lieutenant Newland reporting, sir.'

For a few seconds the general rubbed flattened palms over closed, weary eyes. 'Ah yes, Newland. Well, you're a lieutenant no longer.' He picked up a paper and scanned it. 'You're the only West Point man in E Troop and you've seen more action than most. Come dawn, we've got a fight on our hands and we need fully trained officers. Your senior officer is missing, presumed fallen in battle, so I'm promoting you to captain in his place. You'll be in command of E Troop. That'll be all, Captain.'

'Yes, sir,' Newland said, snapping a sharp salute.

As the general passed the paper to an orderly and returned to discussion with his senior staff, the new captain about-turned.

The corporal pulled back the flap for him to effect his exit and Newland stepped outside to breathe deep of the night air. At last his background was being appreciated. There was such a thing as natural justice after all.

It just needed a helping hand.

2

The next day was a different story. Not only were the numerical odds now in the North's favour, the death of the Confederate's leading general had demoralized the enemy.

And so the fighting was renewed — with a ferocious counter-attack. Although the Southerners managed at one stage to stop the Union advance it was only temporary. Into a second day of fighting they were exhausted and facing fresh opponents. As the Union men had done the day before, it was now the turn of Confederates to put all their efforts into fleeing.

★ ★ ★

For two days the Murdoch family had been aware of the distant noise of gunfire. But during the afternoon of the second day it had become much louder.

With Corinth being a fortified stronghold of the CSA and their little house being on the outskirts of the town they were used to the sight of soldiers. However, late in that afternoon they beheld a sight new to them — fleeing Confederate troops. Some with guns, some without. Some intact, others bloodied and staggering or being helped by comrades.

Their daughter Cathy, full of the curiosity of an eight year old, had pushed her nose against the window pane to view the passing, sorry-looking multitude.

'Mummy, mummy, why can't I watch?' she said as Lisbeth pulled her away, not for the first time.

'Bad things are going on out there,' her mother said. 'Things not for the eyes of gentlefolk and especially gentle-ladies.' She didn't give the more important reason that was worrying her: her fear that bullets might start flying.

Out of earshot of the young child, the couple had debated the prospect of taking themselves to flight but had decided that, potentially, staying or leaving were fraught with equal dangers.

'It's not fair,' Cathy said, slumping sullenly in a chair, hugging her doll. 'Look, papa is watching. Isn't he gentlefolk?'

Partly masked by a curtain, Caldor Murdoch was monitoring events. A doctor, he had had his bag standing on the table for a long time in readiness for being of assistance. Like many, he had been shocked by the sudden escalation of events that had thrown Americans into deadly war with other Americans. Like many civilians, he was not sure that war was the way to resolve difficulties. A grey-haired man, much older than his wife, he had not been eligible to volunteer. But even if he had been younger he might not have put himself forward for, like many southerners, he was still not sure where his sympathies lay.

But he knew where his duties lay.

When he saw an injured man crash through their picket fence, he grabbed his bag and dashed outside. The man had a blood-stained rag around his head.

'Let me have a look at that for you,' he said dropping on one knee. 'I'm a doctor.'

The man, a boy of no more than sixteen, looked at him with eyes that had already seen more than many of his age. 'Thanks, doc, but I'd rather get to Corinth and have my wounds tended there.'

'Let me at least clean it and apply a clean bandage.'

'There ain't time. Just help me to my feet and I'll be on my way.'

The doctor complied and watched the youngster stagger off. The sound of gunfire spurred him to move and he returned to the house. Cathy ran out to greet him.

'You shouldn't be outside,' her father reprimanded.

'I couldn't stop her,' Lisbeth said. 'Come here, Cathy.'

'Let me carry your bag,' the child said. She took her father's bag, dropping her doll, and marched proudly back into the house. It was all just a game to her.

As the sun began to set, the fleeing soldiers increased in number. And the gunfire got louder. Then in the distance Murdoch saw the first of the Union men.

Suddenly the occupants all jumped when a bullet shattered a window pane.

'We've got to make Cathy safe,' the man said, looking around.

'I know,' Lisbeth said. 'In the store.'

It was a wooden-frame house but long ago someone had increased its storage capacity by constructing a small underground store.

'Yes, just the thing,' he said.

'Now it's going to be dark,' Lisbeth said, taking the girl's hand, 'but you're going to be a brave girl, aren't you? It's small and cosy. It won't be for long and mummy and daddy will be here.'

Once the child was safely ensconced, Caldor turned off the oil-lamps and the couple returned to different vantage points at windows. The colours of the uniforms were now equally blue and grey. It was clear the operation was taking on the nature of a mopping-up operation.

Union horseman were overtaking running Confederates and slashing at them with their sabres. Others were being picked off by the long rifles of infantrymen.

'It's horrible,' Lisbeth said, turning away.

'I think they're getting their own back for the drubbing they got yesterday,' he said. 'The reports of casualties are unbelievable. It was the biggest carnage yet by all accounts.'

A grey-clad man crumpled to the ground near the house and Caldor grabbed his bag once more.

'No,' Lisbeth shouted, 'it's too dangerous.'

'I can't just stand by,' he said and dashed outside again. He kept his head low as bullets whizzed this way and that. At the man's side, he examined where the bullet had struck. It was in the chest and the expanding stain testified that the wound was bleeding profusely. 'I'll staunch that,' he said, opening his bag.

The zone in which the Murdoch house stood had been allocated to E Troop. Captain Newman, newly-equipped with horse and sabre, was relishing the vanquishing of a foe who for the past year had had the upper hand. He harsh-reined his horse to a swerving standstill near the house.

'Trooper,' he called, pointing at the doctor he had just caught sight of, 'stop that man aiding the enemy.'

The passing soldier swung the butt of his rifle, smashing it against the doctor's head. Caldor slumped over his patient.

'No, no,' Lisbeth screamed, running from the house.

Newman swung his horse round again and yelled at other troopers. 'Raze that place to the ground!'

'No, you can't!' she screamed, running at him. 'My child's in there!'

He may or may not have heard her words above the gunfire and cacophony of shouting, but it was immaterial because he ignored her anyway, simply shouting, 'The area's got to be cleared!'

He swung his horse against her, buffeting her to the ground. In the fall her head crashed against a stone and she lost consciousness.

★ ★ ★

When she came to, she could feel the heat from the burning house.

'Help!' she screamed but there were few to hear. The routing and slaughter had moved on. She glanced back to where she had last seen her husband but there was only the figure of the now dead soldier.

Hands against her face she ran to the door but had to retreat from the searing inferno. Something pumped through her brain, nature's way of sealing her from catastrophic events, and she collapsed once more.

★ ★ ★

Regaining consciousness a second time, she was numb. It was morning and light; but all she could sense was the acrid smell of smoke. She got to her knees and looked at the smouldering remains of their house, a house that had been turned into a burning coffin for her daughter. She rose and, like an automaton, walked to where the door had been. Through the embers she could see the hole of the burnt-out store closet.

But something stopped her going any further and investigating the contents of the death-trap.

Blank-faced she started walking

backwards until she stumbled on something. She looked down. Cathy's doll.

$$\star \quad \star \quad \star$$

The sprawl of tents was not difficult to find. With the doll dangling from her hand, she approached the sentry.

'I want to see your commanding officer.'

'Captain Newland?'

'If that's his name.'

'I don't think — '

But she whisked on past him.

'Ma'am, ma'am,' he protested, following her for a few steps but reluctant to leave his post.

'Captain Newland,' she demanded of the next soldier in her path, who happened to be a sergeant.

'Yes, ma'am?' He was uncertain of the circumstances but responded to the determination in her voice. 'This way.'

He showed her to a tent and opened the flap. Before he could announce her she had pushed past him. She recognized the man as the officer on the horse — the man who had barked the fateful orders.

'Why have you killed my little Cathy?' she demanded.

Captain Newland looked up. 'What the hell are you talking of, woman?' He snapped a look at the sergeant. 'And who let . . . ?'

'The house you ordered to be burnt down yesterday,' she interrupted through gritted teeth. 'My Cathy was in it. My darling Cathy.'

He pondered. Then he vaguely recalled the episode. 'Ah, yes. The house — with the doctor.' There was no emotion. Face and voice like granite, no remorse showing in either. 'Yes, I remember. If there was child involved — regrettable, ma'am.'

'Regrettable?' she shouted. 'Is that all? Is that word adequate for what you have perpetrated?'

'Regrettable,' his cold voice echoed. 'But these things happen in war.' He threw a glance at the other soldier. 'Sergeant, remove this female from camp.'

And he returned to his paperwork.

The sergeant gripped her arm and firmly escorted her between the tents, past the sentry to the periphery of the encampment.

'The prisoners that were taken yesterday — where are they?' she asked.

The sergeant looked at her. He knew nothing of the woman other than she had lost a child. He had children of his own. He looked around to check he wasn't being seen divulging information to a potential enemy. Then whispered, 'As far as I know, ma'am, all prisoners are being congregated at Pittsburg Landing.'

* ★ *

At Pittsburg Landing there was a regular line of boats crossing the Tennessee. Prisoners, roughly bound with rope were being led single file towards the bank. Her task of identification was made easier because most of the captives wore the grey uniform of the Confederacy.

It took time but eventually she espied her husband. Already he looked different from the man she knew. His clothes were soiled; and he shuffled in a subjugated fashion along the line, as though accepting his lot.

She swept down to the landing under the bemused scrutiny of their blue-uniformed overseers.

'Caldor,' she said, as she got close.

He turned bewildered. 'Lisbeth, is that you?'

'We haven't much time,' she went on. 'Do you know where they are taking you?'

'There's talk of Alton, the prison camp up on the Mississippi.'

She pondered. 'Near St Louis?'

'Yes.'

'St Louis . . . you remember Cousin Hetty? We visited her once at her place in St Louis. I'll make my way there.'

'How's Cathy?'

She gripped his arm. 'Caldor . . . she's dead.'

Before she could register his response a soldier bellowed, 'No talking to prisoners!'

'Remember — Cousin Hetty's!' she shouted as someone grabbed her and dragged her away.

But the soldier was too late. The brief exchange had been enough for them both to receive the information they needed.

3

'My officers tell me you are a doctor.'

Caldor Murdoch was standing between a private and corporal in front of the colonel's desk. The journey to Alton Federal Military Prison had been long and arduous via foot, wagon and railroad. In between stages there had been stretches of mind-fatiguing waiting, roped or chained. He had long since given up protesting his innocence. The original pretext of 'giving aid and succour to the enemy' was long forgotten and he was now simply a Confederate prisoner like the rest.

It was the colonel who was asking the question.

Murdoch nodded. 'I am so qualified.'

'Sir,' the officer snapped.

'I am so qualified, *sir.*'

'And that means you put the welfare

28

of your fellow man before other considerations?'

Murdoch felt like saying, 'Yes, and it's the practice of that principle that is responsible for my present circumstances.' Instead he said, 'We call it the Hippocratic oath.'

He deliberately omitted the 'sir' but the colonel let it pass. 'Be that as it may, I will tell you two things of which you will already be aware. One, we are seriously understaffed on all fronts, especially medical. Two, we have an outbreak of smallpox in the camp. So, if you will swear an oath — equal to your precious Hippocratic words — that you will not use your privileged position to the advantage of the Confederacy, I propose to make you a trustee. In your case, that means helping my own medical staff in the pursuance of their duties. It also means that, for a prisoner, you will have relative freedom of movement. But, I reiterate, you are not to abuse the privilege. Is that understood and agreed?'

'Yes, sir.'

'Very well.' He waved a finger to one of the soldiers. 'Corporal, take this man to Major Hickie.'

★ ★ ★

For the first time in months, Murdoch found himself in the company of what he saw as a civilized man in the shape of Major Hickie, the camp's chief doctor. A professional, the man had one concern: the well-being of those in his charge.

Another benefit for the prisoner, he had access to washing facilities and could recapture a modicum of cleanliness in his condition and appearance. His duties involved tending to wounds, participating in crudely equipped operations and supervising the growing number of smallpox cases.

Up till now his experience of Federal military had been restricted to men barking orders at him and pushing him around. His new, relatively elevated, position brought him into contact with a wider range of Yankee soldier, reflecting the spectrum of ordinary life. The good, the bad and the medium. Among the bad was Lieutenant Stringer, a harsh man who didn't recognize the difference between zealousness and sadism.

A week on, Murdoch was accompanying a burial detail — they used pits at the extremity of the camp for mass burials, out of sight of the bulk of the inmates — when he was overcome with fatigue. His age, the privations of the journey along with the long working day to which he was now subjected compounded to make him perpetually weak and tired. It was dusk and, unseen, he lay behind a mound to rest. And, inevitably, rest became sleep . . .

When he awoke, it was dark. He hauled himself wearily to his feet and peered through the darkness. There was some activity at the pit.

The problem of disposing of dead victims of smallpox was how to bury them without touching the bodies. One way was to throw a loop around the corpse and bed, tie the other end to a horse and lead the animal around the pit. When the body and bed had fallen in, the rope was cut. But horses were becoming as scarce a commodity as anything else.

A second way was in the use of 'immunes'. These were people — either soldiers or prisoners — who had succumbed to the disease and had survived. As a result they couldn't catch the illness again. Snag was, such people were scarcer than horses.

When he was in charge of burial detail Lieutenant Stringer had his own way of handling the problem. He was nothing if not efficient. You took a couple of prisoners and had them handle the bodies. When they had finished their gruesome task you simply slit their throats, pushed them in the pit and covered it over before anyone noticed. It was not only effective, but doing the throat-cutting himself satisfied some twisted craving inside. He had sated his depraved need in this way for some time. None knew, save his two lackeys. Needless to say he would face the severest of punishments should he be found out. Even in war, the army had standards.

As his eyes adjusted to the darkness, Murdoch could make out Lieutenant Stringer in charge of an interment. A body and stretcher were dumped unceremoniously in the hole by a couple of prisoners. To his amazement he saw the lieutenant draw a long knife from a scabbard and slash at the throat of one of the men. The other shouted something but Stringer, with hands suitably gloved for the purpose, meted out the same swift death.

After the two extra corpses had been booted into the hole, the lieutenant turned to give the order to fill in when he caught sight of Murdoch.

'You — here!' he bellowed.

Murdoch thought of running, but where?

He shuffled over to the officer.

'What did you see from over there?' Stringer snapped.

So incensed was Murdoch at the barbarity of the man that he neglected caution and blurted out, 'Enough.'

'Enough?' the lieutenant snapped. He grabbed a rifle from one of the corporals and slammed the butt into Murdoch's chest. 'Enough to do what?'

'Enough to see you on a charge for murder — Lieutenant Stringer,' Murdoch wheezed, gripping the side of his chest. He didn't have to be a doctor to figure one of his ribs was broken. 'Either in a military court now or in a civilian court after this damn war is over. There's been rumours amongst the prisoners that when you take them out on burial detail, they don't come back. Now I know why.'

It was a fateful outburst and the inevitable happened. 'Grab him,' the lieutenant snapped and drew his blade. 'You ain't telling nobody nothing, reb.'

'You can't kill this reb out of hand,

sir,' one of his buddies countered. 'He's too important. The medics will set up some kind of investigation. That could cause trouble for all of us.'

Stringer delayed with his cutter, then sheathed it. He unbuttoned his holster and whammed Murdoch's skull with the butt. 'Hold him here. He comes to, put him out again.' Then he slipped off into the night.

It was some quarter-hour later that he returned. In the interim he had used a pretext to enter the communications office and, when the attention of the overworked telegraph operator had been temporarily elsewhere, had secreted a document from a pile on the desk.

'We had to put him out again, sir,' one of the men said, tapping his rifle butt.

Stringer nodded and took the stolen message from his pocket. He crumpled it up, flattened it out and folded it. Then he wrenched off one of Murdoch's shoes and rammed in the paper, working it around to pick up the stain and smell of the man's foot.

At that moment Murdoch started coming to again. The lieutenant waved the shoe and document in front of the man's wavering eyes. 'What have we here?' he snarled. He opened the paper. 'Hell's teeth — details of Federal troop deployments.'

'I don't know anything about it,' the injured man mouthed.

'I've never heard a spy say anything else,' Stringer sneered. 'OK, Johnny Reb, this is enough to have you up against a wall and shot.'

He smashed Murdoch across the face with the shoe. 'Get him to the stockade while I draw up a report. He'll be out the way by noon tomorrow.'

The soldiers hauled him to his feet and began to drag him away. They were just clear of the burial area when Major Hickie espied them from a distance.

'I'm looking for the trustee Murdoch,' he shouted. 'Have you seen him?'

'Got him here, sir.'

'What's happened?'

'Damn reb is a Confederate agent, sir.' Stringer took out the crumpled message. 'Used his privileged position to gain access to classified information — see here.'

Hickie took the paper, cursorily scanned it and handed it back. 'Incredible.'

He looked over the prisoner. 'He's in bad shape.'

'Gave us a bit of an argument, sir, before we finally found the document hidden in his shoe. Taking him to the stockade.'

The major bent forward and peered more closely at Murdoch's battered face. 'You're not taking this man anywhere, lieutenant. He is badly injured, a condition which makes him my responsibility.'

'He deserves shooting, sir, like all reb spies.'

'Until he is fit to face a firing squad he comes under my jurisdiction.' He gestured to the soldiers propping up the slack figure. 'This man's place is in a hospital bed. You two, bring him with me.'

4

High above the town of Brownsville the bell at the top of the tower of Santa Marguerita's clanged its call to the faithful. The bell was the loudest thing ever heard in the town. No guns, no artillery. At the southernmost tip of Texas, Brownsville was far away from the sounds of war.

As the bell stopped ringing, Sheriff McGann saw the stagecoach rumble round the corner and lurch to a stand-still. He looked at his watch. On time for a change. He studied the passengers as they descended. Made his job easier if he kept tabs on who was coming into town. He made a mental note of the one face new to him, the rest being locals.

He sauntered across the drag as a man on top of the vehicle threw a parcel down to his driving partner.

Newspapers bound in string. The receiver passed them to a waiting storekeeper who knifed through the binding and passed the top copy to the sheriff.

'Thanks, Fred,' the lawman said and parked his backside on a boardwalk seat.

He straightened out *The St Louis Despatch* and noted the date. Only sixteen days old. Hah, the benefits of modern transport. He cast his eyes over the front page. It talked of some battle at Williamsburg. Like most people in town he was only vaguely interested; in fact as uninterested as most people in Texas. The blood-letting up north had been going on a long time before Texas had joined the Confederacy — as the last state to join — and its eventual signing to the cause had been reluctant. He flicked through the rest of the paper, then folded it up carefully for later scrutiny.

★　★　★

Down on the wharf Captain Vanhal was supervising the unloading of timber from up-river. One thing the war had done was increase trade for Brownsville and its sister city Matamoros across the river — cotton going out, guns coming in. And that had meant more buildings being erected — and so more freighting of timber for the bluff German skipper.

The Rio Grande couldn't take ornate floating palaces like the mighty Mississippi but American and Mexican shallow draught steam packets had been plying their way up and down-stream for decades and Vanhal's was one of them.

He was just finishing a deal with a merchant when there was a cracking sound, a thump and a yell. A timber load had become loose on the small crane that was swinging the stuff to the quay and some of the planking had come away. He dashed to the scene. Under the fallen load was his helmsman, Old Man Jessop, grimacing and groaning.

'Fetch the doc,' the skipper shouted as he dashed over to the stricken man.

Minutes later, the load had been eased off the hapless fellow and he had been carried moaning away from the scene.

'Both legs broke,' the doctor said. 'Bad breaks too by the look of it.'

Hearing the diagnosis, one of the dock-hands dashed up the hill and scampered along the main drag towards the Dirty Dollar Saloon.

Inside, Swampy Morgan was not as drunk as he would like to be. Known by all potential employers in town as a thieving drunk, he was unemployed and somewhat deficient with regard to the spending stuff.

He was staring at the dregs in a glass when the dock-hand came through the batwings. The man made his way over to his friend and dropped into a seat beside him.

'Thought you'd like to know. Cap'n Vanhal is shy of a helmsman for his next trip.'

'What's happened to Old Man Jessop?'

'Just bust a leg unloading.'

'Naw, he won't take me on. I've had too many run-ins with the big Kraut.' He stared back at his empty glass. 'Still, no harm in trying.'

'Don't I get drink for telling you?'

'I'm skint. Tell you what — if I get took on I'll get you a drink on payday.'

The other scowled. Apart from his other deficiencies, Swampy Morgan had no memory when it came to favours.

Down on the wharf Morgan presented himself to the Captain. 'Hear you need a wheelman.'

The captain muttered something in German, then: 'I ain't that bad off.' He concluded various dealings around the dock, made some enquiries, then returned to his boat.

Morgan was still at the riverside, sitting on a barrel.

The skipper was in a cleft stick. Through drainage upstream the Rio

Grande was increasingly at low water. This not only meant new obstacles appearing above water level but hidden sandbars, previously no threat, were now more dangerous. It took an experienced helmsman to navigate a craft as big as his and there was only a handful in town. All, save one, were fully occupied somewhere up river.

The only one available was the monkey sitting on the barrel looking at him. Morgan knew his stuff all right but couldn't keep off the liquor which led to problems aboard and Vanhal had sworn never to use him gain.

He gritted his teeth then called, 'Hey, you, *Dummkopf*.'

Morgan shot over.

'I'll give you one more chance,' the skipper said. 'But remember, no booze, no liquor, no nothing.'

'I swear, boss.'

'Right. We push off in an hour. Go and clean yourself up.' He wafted some fresh air round his nostrils. 'That means get a soak in a tub. I don't cotton to suffering that stench for two weeks.'

'Aye, aye, sir.'

★ ★ ★

Back up the hill the service at the church was over and Father Enrico was at the door blessing and bidding Godspeed to his flock. The last to leave, because of her infirmity, was an old lady with stick.

'I'm so glad you could make it, Mrs Fontaine,' the priest said.

The Fontaines had one of the biggest cotton plantations in the country.

'Oh yes,' she said. 'It is of value both spiritually and physically for me to make the effort.' She patted the hand of the man who was half-supporting her. 'But I wouldn't be able to make it if it wasn't for Jim.'

'You have a good son, there, Mrs Fontaine.'

He watched the son help his mother into the surrey and waved as they departed down the hill. Before closing the door he cast a glance over the quiet town below, saw the specks of people going about their business.

Neither he nor any of the specks knew what was just around the corner.

5

The scream pierced his eardrums. Like jagged lightning, zigzagging through his very being, stabbing his stomach, slicing his nerves.

Somewhere a surgeon's saw was hacking off some poor bastard's arm or leg. Chloroform was in short supply so even if you got the benefit of it, you didn't get enough to render unconsciousness, just a bare amount to take some of the edge off the pain. At one time he'd thought he would get used to the sounds of agony, but he hadn't.

From his thin palliasse on the hard planking, he watched the ward-master completing his rounds. Every now and again the man would tie a disc to a patient's ankle.

Calder Murdoch glanced around the ramshackle warehouse they called a hospital, before laying down his head once more. He closed his eyes and thanked God he had been passed over again. As a one-time doctor himself he knew he had recovered enough to be reclassified — and when he was classified as 'healthy' . . .

But the ward-master wasn't concerned with such matters at the moment. The purpose of the man's current round was to identify new cases of smallpox. For the purpose he carried a bunch of wooden discs painted yellow. Each was looped with a thong which was used to tie to a patient diagnosed with pox. The ward-master was an 'immune', one of the few to have contracted and survived the disease, and therefore incapable of succumbing to the illness again. The services of such men were invaluable to the medics.

Murdoch opened his eyes and, through the legs of the adjacent cot, resumed watching the white-coated officer making his inspections.

Those who were lucky had cots. But

for many, even that wasn't as luxurious as it might be, as there were two Confederates to a bunk. Such patients were not only cramped, but having to lie nose to tail, each had to endure the close proximity of the other's stinking feet.

Caldor Murdoch was alive because of the crazy logic of war. Lieutenant Stringer and his buddies had beaten him badly about the head and cracked a rib. Then they would have shot him out of hand had it not been for Major Hickie. Springer was incensed at the intervention. And he still pressed to take Murdoch in charge. He's a spy, he maintained. Both sides reserved the right to shoot spies — that was a code of war too. To shoot him as a spy was one thing, the medic had countered; but now the man was injured he came under the doctor's jurisdiction. You can have him back when he's recovered, he'd said. The crazy logic of war.

So the intervention of some rule-conscious doctor had provided a temporary reprieve. But for how long? And for what? A firing squad when he was better?

And that crux was fast approaching, now that his rib and bruising were on the mend. How long could he maintain the pretence that he was worse than he was? So what were his options? One thing was for sure: if he was to take his fate into his own hands he had to act soon. It would not be long before he was discharged from the hospital. The word of a Union officer would have precedence over Murdoch's claim of innocence. and there was little time for the niceties of debating the legitimacy of evidence. Once on his feet he would be quickly hauled before Springer's firing squad.

And another thing that was sure: there was no escape — with high stockade walls, guards at every door and soldiers patrolling the outer perimeter. The only thing possible was somehow to get out of the filth-pit they called a hospital and into the general compound. He didn't know how many were incarcerated there, but there had to be thousands. Whatever the number, it would be large enough to get lost in. At least for a while.

Having completed his investigations, the ward-master strode up the aisle. He returned the discs to the desk and made his exit. The collection of unholy markers was minus three. It wouldn't be long before other 'immunes' were detailed to move the three unfortunates out to the quarantine compound.

* * *

'What is it, doc?'

The care-worn face before the colonel belonged to Major Hickie. The medic had made an attempt to clean himself up before making his visit to the commander's office but there were still signs of blood on his hands and clothes.

'We're not coping with this smallpox business, sir.'

The colonel crooked his elbow on the

51

desk and leant a weary head on his hand. 'Doc, we're not coping with anything in this place. Overcrowding, food in short supply, inadequate clothing and sanitary facilities. Whatever shit can come down the pike, we get it. Pneumonia, dysentery, rubella. I was trained as a professional soldier. I wasn't given any schooling in managing matters such as these.'

He waved a hand vaguely around. 'You know, when this place was opened as the Illinois State Penitentiary — the first in the state — it was designed to hold a thousand prisoners. Last year, when it was converted as a military prison, its capacity was upped to one and a half thousand.' He jabbed a finger at a piece of paper on his desk. 'At the last count we got over three thousand incarcerated. Three thousand in a pen designed to hold a thousand.'

He jammed a finger at a pile of papers on his desk. 'See those? Copies of requisitions for more men, more food, medical supplies. All unheeded.

Headquarters doesn't even bother to acknowledge receipt of my communications anymore.'

'I'm afraid, colonel, when it comes to smallpox, all that counts for nothing.'

The officer sighed and slumped back in his chair. 'I'm sorry, doc. Forgetting my etiquette. Take a seat and give me details.'

The doctor dropped his own fatigued body in the chair opposite the desk. 'Fact is, increasing numbers per day are succumbing to the illness. Worse, the officer commanding quarantine quarters has just told me they can't take any more. They're overflowing as it is. Now I know you got a heap of problems running a prison of this scale but I can't emphasize enough that if victims aren't quarantined immediately on diagnosis, the disease will spread like a prairie fire through the whole goddamn place. The pox is no respecter of the difference between Reb and Union. If there's a general outbreak, none of your other problems will matter a red nickel.'

'Don't suppose there are any more isolated buildings we can use?'

The doctor shook his head. 'You know there aren't.'

'Then we'll use more tents. What's good enough for Union soldiers should be good enough for Reb prisoners.'

'With respect, sir, more tents aren't the answer. Quarantine is all or nothing. Scattering more tents about the place only increases risk of contagion. You know as well as I that if there is the slightest contact with infected patients, you may as well not have quarantine at all. The whole point about the measure, it has to be an effective seal.'

The colonel grunted. 'Ever since news of the smallpox infection got out, I've had delegations from the town wanting to know what we're doing about isolating the cases from the civilian population.'

'With all due respect, colonel, they have every right to be concerned. Smallpox is one of the four horsemen of the Apocalypse — an horrendous scourge.'

The colonel stared at his desk. 'You a religious man, doc?'

'I do my share of praying.'

'So do I, so do I.' He rose and walked to the window. For a few moments he gazed at the Mississippi flowing slowly past. 'Look at him — Old Man River. He goes by, day in day out, oblivious to the problems of mere mortals.'

He rambled inconsequentially for a few moments — until his voice faded and a change came over his face. A little upstream, there was an island halfway across the river. He pointed. 'That's it. The answer to a prayer. We'll commandeer the island.' His expression turning to a satisfied smile, he looked at the doctor. 'Figure you can't have a more effective isolation than that!'

* * *

Word had filtered back to the ward that smallpox victims were to be shipped out to the island.

Caldor Murdoch got to his feet. Attempting to disguise his improvement he exaggerated his stagger as he moved along the aisle. He reached the table on which were stacked the smallpox discs.

'Need to use the latrine, sir,' he said to the sentry standing near the desk.

The soldier grunted in annoyance and signalled to his fellow-guard at the other end of the building that he was accompanying a patient outside. Then he poked the prisoner with his barrel end to get him moving.

Outside it was cold as dusk was setting in. Murdoch did what he had to do in the stinking hole and made the journey back to the clapboard building. As he passed the desk he feigned to trip, catching the yellow discs as he fell, scattering them on the floor.

'Awkward Reb bastard,' the soldier mouthed. He bent down to reclaim them, muttering, 'Get back to your damn cot, and don't cause any more trouble.'

A minute later Murdoch was under his blanket once more. As he moved to find a comfortable position for his body he felt the reassuring shape of the disc under his jacket. The poor light of the lamp-lit room had simplified his task of claiming and smuggling it as he had grovelled clumsily on the floor.

If the collection of smallpox victims was made before dawn, then that same poor light would help him in the next step of his plan. He waited for a while then, slowly so as not to catch attention, bent himself double so he could tie the thong to his ankle. Finally he pulled the blanket over his head. A blanket over the head was the other indication used by the hospital staff to identify a smallpox victim.

★　★　★

As he hoped, the exercise was conducted in darkness. Also, as he had hoped, the orderlies who came to shift them were from the quarantine section and didn't know him. With no concern for looking at his face they had dumped him on a stretcher and taken him down to the waiting boat.

With 'immunes' being in scarce supply there were only two boatmen and one guard per boat. From under his blanket he watched the spots of light on the prison side of the river get fainter and fainter; and ahead the lights of the newly established quarantine island. The weight of the putrefying cargo had brought the waterline tantalizingly up to the gunwales. At the point of maximum blackness between the bank and island, he slipped over the side, easing himself into the water to reduce splashing. None of the guards or boatmen noticed.

Despite the searing pain of his mending rib he took a deep breath so he could stay under water as long as possible. His teeth jammed together with the coldness. The water was freezing — but it represented freedom.

Lungs bursting, he eased himself

upwards keeping his head back so that only his lips broke the surface. There was no noise other than the sounds of the river. He hadn't been seen.

Now the focus of his attention changed: could he survive the cold? Would his emaciated body even have the energy to get to a river bank?

He felt the whip of the current as he fought to make life-saving strokes.

★ ★ ★

Lieutenant Stringer strutted down the narrow aisle studying the patients. Agitation and frustration showed in the jerkiness of his movements. Where a face was covered by a blanket he used his swagger stick to reveal the man's features.

'Where is the bastard?' he grunted repeatedly.

At the end of his search he stomped to the colonel's office.

'The spy Murdoch — he's gone,' he informed the camp commander.

'Died?' the colonel suggested.

'No record, sir.'

'You think somehow he got himself merged in with the healthy prisoners in the main compound?'

'Doesn't seem so, sir.'

'Maybe he was transferred to the island.'

'They've made a search for him. No sign of him over there.'

'Well, don't know how he's done it but looks like he's managed to get away. If he has, figure he'll try to get south. Get on to Communications. Tell them to circulate his details and description.'

'We can do better than that, sir. Our one piece of luck: he was in a batch who were recorded on a photographic plate. Somewhere we've got a picture of him.'

'Well, locate it, get copies and include it in all communications. And make sure they state he's a spy and can be shot on sight.'

6

Lisbeth Murdoch was awakened by a noise. At first she couldn't understand why the sound had disturbed her. So faint. Like a branch in the wind catching the woodwork. Then, as she lay pondering, she realized *what* it was about the noise that had awakened her. It wasn't the volume; it was the regularity.

Fully awakened, she listened in the darkness. There it was again. Soft, but persistent. It was at the door.

She pulled on a robe and lit a lamp. Slowly she made her way down the stairs and stood by the door. There it was again. It was someone knocking.

'Who is it?' she demanded.

'It's I. Caldor.'

Her jaw dropped. It couldn't be. There was no way he could be freely wandering the streets. But it was her man. Even from behind a door and in a whispered tone the voice of her beloved husband was unmistakable. She threw the bolt. He was leaning exhausted against the jamb. As she opened the door wider, he collapsed into the room. She closed the door and put down the lamp. She dropped to her knees, cradling him, kissing him, repeating his name.

Then there were questions. 'You're wet, cold. What's happened? How did you get here?'

'I escaped,' he croaked.

She glanced at the dying embers of the fire. 'I'll put some logs on the fire. You come and sit while I get a towel and some dry clothes.'

She winced when she was stripping him and saw, with the extra light from the fire, the bruising about his emaciated body. 'My love, you've been beaten.'

He told her his story as he wolfed down bread and stew. About how he had been branded as a spy.

'I'm now doubly glad I could make it to St Louis,' she said when he'd finished.

'Where's Hetty?' he said, glancing around.

'My cousin is staying with her mother in the Carondelet district. Trying to give her some consolation. You remember Tom, her brother?'

He nodded. When visiting with Lisbeth before the war he had been introduced to all of them, but there were so many young men in the family he couldn't recall the Tom she spoke of, but he made no comment.

'Well, he was killed at Willamsburg,' Lisbeth went on. 'So I have the place to myself for the time being. Yes, I'm so glad I came. My original intention in coming was simply to be near Alton camp and close to you. I little dreamt my action would provide a refuge for you in your time of need.'

He nodded, clenched her hand, then said, 'Well, it is that. But the sooner I'm gone the better. Pack me some food,

63

give me some money and I'll be on my way.'

'Oh, Caldor, you're not leaving me now.'

He clenched her hand tighter. 'Listen, Lisbeth, I have to. Having branded me as a spy, they're bound to put a deal of effort into looking for me and there's a strong chance I'll be traced. I can't be found here with you. Whatever they do with me, you'll be branded 'disloyal' — that's the term they use for Southern patriots — and they'll treat you badly. Likely slam you in that scum-hole of Gratiot Street prison they got here. From what I hear that's as bad as the Alton camp.'

'Where are you planning on going?'

'To get as far from Alton and St Louis as I can.'

She thought on his words. 'I'm not going to be parted from you again. Wherever you're going I'm coming with you. And wherever you go you're going to need help getting away.'

'They'll be on the lookout for me.

They've got my image on one of those photography things.'

'Do they know what I look like?'

'I don't think so.'

'Then there's no problem.' For the first time since his arrival a humorous smile crinkled her lips. 'Calder Murdoch, you never cottoned to the idea that you were older than me. Well, now our age differences are going to come in useful. I'll wrap you up and pass you off as my ailing old father.'

She thought some more. 'Hetty's family are all Pro-Secessionists. They know the local circumstances. They'll give us help and some ideas. Maybe know a place where we can hole up or help us to leave.'

Unlike many communities involved in the conflict, St Louis was of deeply divided sentiments, situated as it was between Illinois and Missouri. Although the Union Army was dominant in the city, the city held a large population of pro-Confederate civilians.

He stared into the fire. 'OK, if you're

sure.' Then: 'We'll only take a few things. We'll leave a little money here too. So, if and when they come a-searching, it doesn't look like you've left the place for good.'

Minutes later, Lisbeth was upstairs packing a small case. The first thing she put in it was a small hand-made doll with woollen ringlets.

★ ★ ★

So as not to arouse suspicions by acting furtively they walked quite openly along the streets in the glare of the gas lighting of which the city was so proud. Martial law had been proclaimed throughout the metropolis and they hadn't walked very far when they were stopped and questioned by a unit of the 54th Massachusetts Troop. The couple's story was they were father and daughter on the way to visit a sick relative.

'So far so good,' Murdoch muttered when out of earshot after they were permitted to continue on their way. 'They're not searching us as vigorously as they could, and their questioning seems pretty routine — so I figure news hasn't yet reached them of my escape.'

Dawn was breaking as they passed the Carondelet shipyards where the Federal gunboats were being constructed.

'Not far now,' he said.

Eventually Lisbeth located the house she was looking for, a little distance along the Des Peres River.

* * *

Hetty and her family were glad to see them.

'You're one of the family,' one of the many brothers said when Caldor had related his experiences, 'and we deem the chance to assist you as an honour, sir. Do not worry. Our responsibility is to see that you are safe.'

He gestured around the room. 'Trouble is I don't think this place will be safe for you for long. The city is teeming with what they call 'volunteer detectives', a fancy name for civilians who are Federal sympathizers. The sneaking weasels can be anybody, you just don't know who they are — store-owners, next-door neighbours. They pass on anything suspicious and it could happen that one of them tells the Feds about Lisbeth staying at Hetty's. And that would lead them here. Consequently, if they are intent on pursuing you, the two of you could be conspicuous. Figure the best thing is for you to get out of St Louis altogether.'

'Any ideas?' Caldor asked.

'Well the Union controls the river and all main highways and trails.' He pondered on the matter, then added, 'Except one. How do you cotton to a life in the great outdoors?'

'What's on your mind?'

'With ordinary folk trying to escape the hostilities, the flow of wagons westward has become a flood. From here they take the trail alongside the

Missouri and join the bigger outfits at the frontier post at Independence. Then it's the Sante Fe Trail and all points west. You don't have any money for a wagon and supplies?'

'No,' Lisbeth said. 'We lost everything when the house was burned down.'

'I've got savings,' Hetty's mother said. 'You can see it as a loan until you get back on your feet.'

Her son raised his eyebrows. 'It's not going to be cheap, Ma. The mass exodus has jacked up the prices of all the necessaries.'

'Don't you fret,' the old lady said. 'I can cover what's required.'

'Very well,' her son nodded. 'That's settled. Now, all the chandlers and provisioning stores are out on the western side of town — that's where the wagon trains start. There are always Union men down there watching the comings and goings so one of us will go down and buy a wagon and make the necessary purchases. That way, you

69

won't be drawing attention to yourselves as a couple trying to get out of
town quick.'

He smiled. 'Sometimes there's over a
hundred wagons in a caravan. Once
we've got you on your way the
bluebellies will be looking for needles in
a haystack.'

Caldor looked at his wife. 'We're
gonna be cowboys.'

She smiled. 'Anything you say,
pardner.'

★ ★ ★

Lieutenant Stringer gave orders for
soldiers to cover the back door and
windows. 'Anybody tries to escape
— shoot first and ask questions later.'

Then two beefy troopers used the
weight of their shoulders in unison
against the front door until it crashed
open.

Pistol levelled, the officer stepped
into the interior. He listened, detected
nothing. 'Search the place.'

He went outside, eyed a pile of garbage in the yard. He turned bits over with his boot, eventually exposing dirty, bloodstained clothes. Back inside, his men had ascertained the house was empty.

'He's been here,' he said.

'Lots of stuff about, sir,' one of the men said. 'Doesn't look like they've left for good.'

'Means nothing. They've skipped all right.' He walked over to the seemingly dead fire. He put his hand close to the ashes in the grate and detected the vestiges of warmth. 'And can't have been gone more than a few hours.'

★   ★   ★

They were some dozen miles out of St Louis. Lisbeth sat on the seat of the covered wagon, reins in hand. Caldor had been driving when they had set out but weakness had overtaken him and now he was resting under the shelter of the cover.

The depot on the western side of town with its stores and warehouses had had all the provisions necessary for an overland trek. As planned one of Hetty's brothers had made all purchases on their behalf at the depot — food, necessary utensils and tools right down to a Spencer carbine — and, despite the surveillance of Union men, there had been no trouble kitting them out with a fourhorse wagon. To the teamster heading the train they had just been another handful of dollars to add to his purse.

They were at the tail end of the caravan, a mile long, a motley assortment of prairie schooners, canvasbacked wagons, buckboards, that were already taking on a film of dust.

Axles creaked, and the paraphernalia slung under the vehicles — water-kegs, churns and buckets — clattered and clunked. Then, above the familiar amalgam of sound, Caldor heard something different. The regular clop of cantering horses. And it sounded like they were coming up from the rear. He moved his weak body to the back of the vehicle and parted the canvas flaps.

The wagon train was strung out between a couple of ridges and a unit of blue uniforms was coming into view over the ridge behind them. He closed the flaps until there was a mere crack through which he could maintain his vigil. He watched the horsemen approach and pass, then he moved up forward to observe their progress along the train ahead.

'Trouble,' he whispered to Lisbeth. 'That's the lieutenant at the head of them bluebelly troopers.'

'Lieutenant?'

'Yeah, from Alton. Lieutenant Stringer,' he explained. 'The meanest cuss who ever put on a uniform — of any colour. The one branding me an agent.'

'What are they doing out here?'

'Dunno. Mebbe heading out to Independence like we are.'

'Somehow I don't think so. What'll we do?'

'Well, nothing to arouse suspicions for a start. Let's wait and see.' He eased himself back down into the wagon but kept his head just high enough to see ahead over the seat.

In time the train began to slow down and finally came to a standstill with the head out of sight over the next ridge. Lisbeth heaved on the brake while Caldor maintained his vigil below her. Eventually one of the caravan's outriders appeared, riding back along the column and shouting something in turn to each wagon. When he reached the end of the train he wheeled his horse around. 'Bit of a delay, ma'am,' he said to Lisbeth. 'The military are checking each wagon.'

She wanted to ask if he knew what they were searching for, but she knew that that would be a suspicious question. Instead she tried to make her voice sound as casual as possible and asked, 'How long will the delay be?'

'Dunno, ma'am. Figure it could be some time 'cos they're making a mighty thorough job of it. But I shouldn't worry, ma'am. It'll give our draught animals a rest.' With that he gigged his horse to head back up the train.

'You think they're looking for you?' she asked her husband when the man was well out of earshot.

'Could be looking for anybody, but one thing's for sure — I'll be on the list somewhere.'

He looked back. The ridge they had come over wasn't too far back. 'I'm going to make a run for it. If they find me with you, God knows how they'll treat you. It's going to take them some time to work their way down to us so, if I can get back over that ridge, at least I'll be out of sight for a spell. That'll give me the opportunity to find somewhere to hide.'

'If you go, we go together. I'm not being parted from you again, Caldor Murdoch. And anyway, you're not well enough to be out here on foot by yourself.'

'It's the only thing, Lisbeth.'

'No it's not. The hollow beyond the ridge back there is deep enough to hide the wagon for a time too.'

'Are you sure you want to chance it?'

'Of course.'

'OK. But we can't just turn the wagon round and leave the caravan without saying something to the folks ahead. They're going to tell the soldiers we've broken away from the train anyway.' He thought for a moment. 'Tell 'em your old man's taken a turn for the worse and you're heading back to St Louis to get medical attention. With a bit of luck, once we're over that ridge we stand a chance of turning off the trail and getting clear. Then, if we can get out of sight, even if the Union men are suspicious they'll continue looking for us on the trail back to St Louis.'

Lisbeth went ahead and, in suitably

76

distraught fashion, relayed the suggested story to the occupants of the next wagon. An elderly matronly woman came and had a look at Caldor who groaned and exaggerated his condition so that she had to agree it was probably better that they return so he could receive proper medical attention. Then a couple of men helped Lisbeth turn their four-horse team. The folks wished the Murdochs well and the wagon headed back, ostensibly towards St Louis.

Once over the ridge Caldor joined his wife on the seat and took the reins. At the base of the shallow valley he glanced back to make sure they still hadn't been seen and swung the wagon south across the grassland. With the trace-chains rattling the horses made heavy going on the virgin ground, but their progress was aided by the gentle downward slope. Eventually the terrain levelled to join a creek. The creek bottom was heavily timbered providing ample cover from the trail.

'As long as they don't see our wagon ruts leaving the trail, we should be OK,' Caldor said as they travelled between the creek and the trees.

His wife clutched his arm. 'It's going to be a long haul. Think you can manage it?'

'I'm feeling better already.'

'When you feel tired, I'll take over again. Heading south to our own lines and our own people will be just as good for us as trying to disappear out west. And once we're across the Mason-Dixon line you'll be truly safe.'

★   ★   ★

Lieutenant Stringer was standing before his commanding officer. 'When we rode out there to check the wagon train I wasn't sure Murdoch was on it, sir. But I am sure now.' He walked over to the map on the wall. 'We learned that a wagon at the tail end left the train while we were conducting the search. A wagon with a man and a woman in it.

Told folks they were heading back to St Louis. But we saw no wagon fitting the description on the return trip. That means they turned off.' He stabbed the map with his finger. 'We stopped the train round about here.' His finger moved an inch along the trail and stopped. 'That means they must have cut off about . . . here.'

He mused on the possibilities. 'Now, they wouldn't have gone north because they would hit the Missouri. Anyway, north would be enemy territory for the critter so I figure they'd have no option but to head south. It's rough country for a wagon but if they make one of the regular trails — such as the Butterfield stage route — the running will be easier.'

'What are you leading up to?'

'I'd like your permission to light out after him.'

The colonel rubbed eyes weary from lack of sleep. 'Are you sure one man merits all this fuss?'

Stringer's mind raced. From a

military point of view the pissant didn't merit a red cent. But the man had meant what he said about bringing the lieutenant to book now or after the war. Being an educated man, the doctor would have the clout to get important people to listen to him. Stringer could not rest easy until the man was permanently silenced. Besides, when he started something he always saw it through to the end.

But none of this would be relevant to the colonel. He had to make a strong military case so he said, 'In Rebel eyes the bastard's got status, sir. It'd be a kick in their teeth if we could apprehend him and dole out his due desserts. Also it'll show other Confederate agents we mean business. Not to mention being good for the morale of our men too.'

'You think it's that important?'

'Begging your pardon, sir, the man was trying to smuggle out information on our troop deployments.'

'Very well. Think you could do it?'

'One thing I do know — I can move faster than a wagon.'

'It'd have to be alone. I can't release any men.'

'Even better, sir.'

'Very well, you have my permission. Keep me informed. And good luck.'

7

Three weeks on and they were well into Arkansas. From time to time they would catch sight of Union soldiers but they were only stopped once. Not having shaven, Caldor carried a beard, while his time in captivity had added more grey hairs so that his appearance had now changed somewhat. Whether it was this or the fact that news of him had not yet travelled south, they aroused no suspicion.

They had one aim: to cross the border into Texas where they would be in Confederate territory and could look for a place to settle away from Union eyes. Their progress was slow but steady. Their supplies were running low and they purchased food from town stores and way-stations whenever they could as they travelled, but the war was pushing prices up drastically. At night they would break off dead limbs from cottonwoods to make a fire. Sometimes they were invited into a ranch house or stagecoach station to sleep.

★ ★ ★

Time and miles passed. Once they'd crossed the border into Texas they began to feel safe for the first time. Their focus now became the more mundane matter of deciding where to settle. So occupied had they been with escape they had not given much thought to their final destination. So one evening round the fire, they'd got out their map and began making plans like an ordinary married couple once more. Eventually they fixed on Abilene. Both were strangers to the territory but they had heard it was a growing town and there was bound to be scope for a doctor they figured. And if they didn't like it they could always move on when the war was over. So, two days later when they cut a trail heading west they took it.

It was a fine day. Caldor had taken the first spell with the traces and then they had broke for lunch. After the meal he was tired and on the resumption of their journey he had taken to his bed while Lisbeth handled the team.

They had proceeded a few miles when Lisbeth espied a couple of men beside the trail ahead.

'Soldiers,' she said.

As the wagon neared the men moved to the middle of the trail and one waved a rifle in a gesture for them to stop. She was near enough to see the grey of their bedraggled uniforms.

'We're OK. They're Confederate.' But her fatigued husband was still sleeping and didn't hear.

'Howdy, miss,' one said approaching as she stayed the wagon.

'Afternoon,' she replied, scanning the distance. There were no others to the horizon in any direction. 'Where's your unit?'

The man sniggered at his companion who had now joined them and was leaning on his rifle watching the exchange. 'Unit she says. Lady, you're looking at it. What's left of it. Didn't stand a chance.'

'The war's spread to Texas?'

'Lady, it's not only spread to Texas — the old Lone Star is collapsing.'

Her heart sank.

'We got our asses whupped out near Sante Fe,' he went on. 'Out west, the Colorado Volunteers are streaming down like rats. And last we heard the Feds are marching in from the east like there's nothing to stop 'em. It's over for Texas.'

He leant close. 'Only thing now for me and my pal is to shuck these uniforms and get ourselves into some plain duds. Kinda dangerous wearing grey in Texas now.'

'Yeah,' his friend added. 'Then we'll make out like we never held a rifle in our born lives and head home to our kin.'

'So what clothes you got that we can, er, borrow, ma'am?' the chief spokesman asked.

'I'm afraid I haven't got anything that would be of help.'

'Oh yes, you do,' he snapped and he yanked her off the seat so that she stumbled and fell on her knees. 'If you ain't got clothes, you got money, food.'

The other slung his gun aside and spun her over. He straddled her body and mauled at her breasts. 'And you got something else we're gonna help ourselves to.'

His companion pulled him back. 'No. That can wait. We'll see what she's got of value in the wagon first. Then we'll have *her* for dessert.'

He walked round to the back of the wagon. 'You keep hold of her while I take a look-see.' He withdrew the retaining clips and dropped the backboard. But he did not expect what his 'look-see' revealed. The black hole of a Spencer.

As the man rocketed backwards with

the explosion, his companion let go Lisbeth and made a grab for his own discarded gun. In other circumstances Caldor's stiffness and weakness would have made him too slow in disembarking from the wagon. But the soldier had deliberately slung his rifle some distance away to remove temptation from Lisbeth. And that was his undoing. Caldor's gun eventually barked again and the soldier took the slug while still prone on the ground. Yards from his gun, his fingers grasped in vain, then ceased to grasp.

Lisbeth leapt up and ran to throw her arms round her staggering husband.

'No, no,' he said, pushing her away. 'Check those creatures are no more threat.'

He slumped to the ground, still holding the Spencer. She checked the men were dead, then joined him and they clasped each other.

'They were animals,' she murmured. 'Our own kind too.'

'War can turn people into savages.'

When they had composed themselves Lisbeth stood up. 'Shouldn't we bury them?'

'No. I don't have the strength to wield a shovel and it will unnecessarily deplete your resources.' His head swivelled. 'Over there, see, that hollow. It'll be enough to dump the bodies in that. They'll be away from the trail. Not that it matters. Nobody will be bothered. They'll just be dismissed as war casualties.'

'I was thinking more of doing the decent thing. Giving them a Christian burial. After all, they're some mothers' sons.'

He grunted. 'They weren't concerned that *you* might be a mother.' He knelt beside one and opened the ammunition bag hanging from the belt. It was full of rings, assorted jewellery and notes, both Confederate and Union. 'See, the scavengers have done a lot of this before. So we'll do to them what they were intending to do to us. Take their valuables. We're running short of the wherewithal as it is.'

'We're not even safe from our own kind,' she said when they had hauled the bodies out of sight and were once more seated in their wagon. 'Let's get away from this evil place as soon as possible. The problem is where to? If Texas is falling it's not going to be the haven we were hoping for.'

'You're right. We can say 'so long' to Abilene. If Federal forces are moving in from both east and west we're gonna have to turn south again. Where's the chart?'

She clambered over the seat into the back of the wagon and came back with their map. She spread it across their laps and they both pondered on it.

'It is my opinion that we should now make for the Rio Grande and cross to Mexico,' she said after a while. 'That is one place where you will be truly safe for the duration.' Her finger traced down the map. 'Looks like we could make the crossing at Brownsville.'

'Yeah.' He looked around. 'The

terrain doesn't look too bad hereabouts. We'll turn off the trail here and if we take a course due south-east we should pick up that southern trail that we left back-aways.'

8

The further south they travelled the browner and drier became the soil. It had been days since they had come across water for the horses. Coming to the shade of some cottonwoods they pulled in.

Caldor looked in the main water keg. 'Barely enough left to dampen lips.' They shared the now familiar ritual of pouring water from the keg into pails for the horses.

After they had taken a drink themselves, he looked once more into the depths of the barrel. 'We got ourselves some trouble if we don't come across water soon.'

Some ten miles on they topped a rise and were happy to see a building beside the trail in the distance. 'Let's hope it's occupied and they got a supply of water,' Caldor said. Lisbeth took the traces and Caldor slipped into the back as was their habit.

As they neared a dog came towards them, barking his challenges.

'Thank God for that,' Lisbeth said when they were closer. 'I can see a water pump.'

By the time she was drawing the wagon to a halt, a man had emerged from the building which bore the label STAGECOACH STATION. 'Howdy, ma'am,' he shouted.

Lisbeth reciprocated the greeting and asked if she could take water.

'Help yourself, ma'am,' he said pointing to the pump and trough. 'I'll give you a hand.'

The dog yapped at the wagon as they began unfastening the first horse.

'Why don't you folks come in for a meal and a rest-up?' the man suggested as they led the horse to the trough.

'Who says there's anyone travelling with me?'

The man looked at the wagon and then back at her. 'Forgive me for being presumptuous, ma'am, but the state of you tells me you've been on the trail a long, long time. Quite a few hundred miles by my reckoning. And even a capable-looking female such as yourself ain't likely to have handled a four-hoss wagon over such a distance all on her ownsome. Besides you look and talk like a sensible woman, the kind of woman who would know such an undertaking ain't sensible — ain't safe for a start.'

She splashed some water over the back of a drinking horse. 'Like you say I'm a sensible woman. Leastways, sensible enough to be able to look after myself.'

The man nodded. 'I don't doubt it, ma'am, but I'll tell you something. Living out here all on my ownsome I've developed a sixth sense. Travellers can break the horizon and even though I ain't looking that way at the time I can feel I got visitors. Then it is my habit to give 'em the once over with my spyglass. When you broke the horizon yonder there was a guy handling the traces.' He pointed to the dog, still yapping at the wagon. 'And Kipper knows someone's in there. That's what he's telling me.'

A hint of embarrassment came to Lisbeth's features. 'You're quite right. There are two of us. It's my ailing father in back.'

The man turned and began walking back towards his shack. 'Get your old feller to help you finish your watering then, like I said, the two of you come over for a meal and a rest-up.'

Caldor overheard the conversation and emerged from the wagon to be greeted by the dog that immediately exchanged barking for a wagging tail. The man bent down and patted the animal before joining his wife in tending to the horses.

★ ★ ★

The man placed steaming coffee mugs in front of them. 'Ain't the best java,

I'm afraid, folks. Good stuff is hard to come by these days, what with the war and all.' They had just finished a very filling meal.

'You care for a smoke, sir?' the man continued. 'Got some Virginy. A mite dry but it fits the bill.'

Caldor bent down and stroked the dog who had taken up residence close to him. 'Don't mind if I do, sir. That's mighty kind.'

Lisbeth rose from the table. 'While you two men-folk do your smoking, I'll wash the platters. It's the least I can do in return for your hospitality.'

The man smiled. 'The first time in a coon's age I had the dishes washed by a female.'

The men built their smokes and exchanged a few words of no consequence. A little later Lisbeth rejoined them to settle down with another cup of coffee.

'Get a lot of folks stopping by,' the man said. 'Some interesting company like your goodselves. Some interesting for other reasons. Like the feller who stopped by the other day. A northerner. Got that fancy way of talking, you know, the way northerners do. Asked me if I'd seen a man and a woman travelling alone in a wagon. Southerners he said they were.'

He paused and his eyes moved from one face to the other but they gave no reaction. 'He was kitted out in trail duds but he was a soldier,' he continued. 'I could tell by his speech and manner.'

He waited again but neither of his guests spoke. He nodded to the dog. 'Kipper there is a good judge of character. He's sure took to you, sir. See the way he's happy in your company, just lying there at your feet. On the other hand, all the time this other feller was here Kipper sat by me — staring at the guy and giving a grunt every now and then. He knew this feller had mean intentions.'

Then he stretched and rose. 'Excuse me, folks. Nature calls.'

Lisbeth waited till he'd gone and whispered, 'That fellow can't be searching for us. He was here *ahead* of us.'

'We must have lost the best part of a week when we turned for Abilene. He could easily have overshot us then.'

She nodded.

'I figure it's Stringer all right,' he added. 'It's too much of a coincidence.' And they left the discussion at that.

'Privy's out back should you need it,' the man said when he eventually returned. He sat down and refilled his coffee mug.

'Now I'm not going to ask any questions,' he continued. 'In these unsettled times it's often the case that the less a body knows the better. But seems to me the Northern military are after a couple of Confederates who have some-hows caused the bluebellies a heap of trouble. Now, I don't mind telling fellow Southerners like yourselves that anybody who has stuck a spoke in the Yankee's wheel gets my dollar. So, in the light of the situation as

I see it, I'm going to make a suggestion.'

'I don't know what this conversation is about,' Lisbeth said. 'How can we be the couple that this fellow is after?'

The man smiled. 'Lady, don't start that game again. A body doesn't hide in a wagon with his trail buddy pretending he isn't there for no good reason. Like I said, I'm not going to ask any questions.'

The couple exchanged glances as the man continued. 'I take it you're heading for Brownsville, maybe to cross the river. Well, that's the direction this guy rode off in. So he'll be waiting for you there. Now, the stage to Brownsville is due in tomorrow. This is its last stop. So, the idea is this: I buy your horses and wagon. I can't give you the going price but I'll give you what I can spare. Then you join the stage. That way you'll look a little less suspicious when you turn up in town.'

9

Sheriff Bill McGann walked past the shirtless slaves heaving bales of cotton out of a warehouse ready for shipment. He continued along the river landing, then rested his rump against a barrel to watch the ferry make its way across the swathe of the Rio Grande. The vessel's progress was slow but he had no urgent appointments. Nothing was urgent in Brownsville. This was Brownsville, Texas, hundreds of miles from the bloody conflict that was occupying his fellow Americans.

There probably wasn't a nation on earth that wasn't represented somewhere in town — from Russians to Chinese. He himself typified the cosmopolitan mix of Texas's most southern town. He was first generation American. His father had been Scottish, his mother Norwegian. After his mother died, his father had married a Mexican from the other side of the river. Hence his sister Doña, who ran a hotel in town, was Mexican-American.

He wasn't normally given to philosophizing but, given all the nationalities around, he couldn't for the life of him figure out why when the big scrapping started — namely, the current war being played out to the north — it had to be between *Americans*.

Anyway, having lived through the Texan War as a child, at the end of the day he saw himself as Texan.

He lit a cheroot and absently contemplated the scene, his mind on nothing in particular. From his vantage point he could just sense the coolness of the river while the scent of bougainvillea blossom filled his nostrils.

Boats of all kinds were moored along the stretch of the riverfront, in places two and three deep: barges, cargo boats, flatboats. With the constant coming and going there were always strange faces about. Mostly river scum, so squabbling and fighting was the norm. However, even though he toted a badge, he didn't see himself as being responsible for their shenanigans. His sole duty with regard to the river rats was to make sure none of them strayed into the genteel part of town where the tradesfolk and cotton planters lived. Besides, when scrapping got serious and somebody got killed, the resulting body would soon be floating down the river. None of his business.

Yes, siree, he had a good life. No trouble. His only aim in life was to build up a nest egg with which he could skedaddle should things heat up. All the war meant to him and his fellow citizens at the moment was news in the *St Louis Dispatch* and other papers that arrived in town weeks after their issue. And of course the war meant a chance to make a few bucks.

But he was a realist. He knew that, if things didn't resolve themselves quickly in those distant places, it would only be a matter of time before even

Brownsville was affected. Texas had kept its nose out things as long as it could. For a start, the Chief Justice of the Supreme Court had made a ruling prohibiting federal interference in states' affairs on slavery. Furthermore, all the signs were that the North would give way on the slavery issue for the sake of peace. So for a while it looked as though that was the end of the trouble.

The first real bad news for the South was when Lincoln got elected to the presidency. During his campaign, anti-slavery had been the linchpin of his platform so the matter was a thing he would stand fast on. And now he was in power there was no way he would countenance the Southern territories of the country having different policies on the slavery issue.

As a result, the State of South Carolina had quickly passed an Ordinance of Secession. A further six states withdrew from the Union and, along with South Carolina, had set up what they called the Confederacy. The new nation had a president, Davis, and a new flag.

But even then Texas had still kept its nose out of the matter. It had been no concern for them — that was until the Confederacy Commissioners had gone to Washington to talk with Lincoln. That had been the turning point for the Lone Star state. It could sit on the fence no longer. When old Abe had sent the Commissioners off with the sounds of his obduracy ringing in their ears, Texas had finally joined the Confederacy.

For a while the war had been a remote thing not impinging on distant settlements like Brownsville. It meant nothing more to its folk than dry newsprint accounts to be talked over in the saloons. They knew their geography and that the Mississippi provided a natural barrier, which restricted the conflict to the eastern states.

In their little settlement of Brownsville by the river there had been scant evidence of military personnel, save for occasional recruiting officers. And their visits had become less frequent with the realization that the westerns states of the Confederacy — and particularly Texas — were still not under immediate military threat from Union forces. The only sign of something being untoward elsewhere on the continent was the increasing number of families moving west and south to escape the strife.

So Texas was having a quiet war.

So far.

He took another draw on his cheroot as deckhands threw out hawsers. Negro dockhands secured the ropes to stanchions on either side of the jetty just as the ferry bumped heavily against it. The massive gangplank was lowered into position and the vessel's few passengers disembarked. Then the first of a train of wagons was hauled ashore. As draught horses were brought forward to be hitched, he yawned and glanced westward. In the distance a steamboat was working her way upstream.

Eventually the last of the wagons was clear of the ferry. He crushed the remains of his cheroot underfoot and was about to step forward and claim his cut — he had a cut of all such trade across the river — when he sensed something was wrong. He paused, not knowing at first what it was. Then he realized what was different. The general noise of activity around him had died down and an eerie quietness had descended on the scene.

The silence was broken by an authoritative voice. 'Nobody move.'

He eased his backside off the barrel and turned. The source of the command was a soldier — a Union soldier — marching down to the water's edge. From the cut of his uniform the intruder looked like a major or something.

The lawman scanned the scene. Jeez, from every point along the riverfront, men in the hated blue were appearing with raised rifles. Where the hell were the Confederate soldiers who were supposed to be protecting the town?

'Sergeant, find out who's in charge of this ferry,' the officer ordered. As his sergeant set about his task, he gestured to some men near him, then pointed to the wagons. 'And you — see what's in them.'

Three soldiers clambered aboard the first wagon and began jabbing at barrel tops with their rifle butts.

'Liquor, sir,' one said eventually, dabbing liquid to his lips. 'Mexican stuff. Looks like tequila. It's all the same in here.'

The officer pointed to the next wagon. 'And that?'

The ritual was repeated. 'Salt, sir,' the soldier concluded.

'All the same there too?' the officer went on.

'There's a tarp underneath, sir.'

'Well, look underneath, soldier,' the officer snapped as his sergeant brought a rotund fellow to his side. The man wore a flat river-cap and his bulky stomach was held in by a thick belt.

The men threw some barrels onto the quay and lifted a tarpaulin. 'Crates, sir.'

'Then break them open, man.'

The watching lawman knew what was coming and edged some yards further away but remained close enough to monitor proceedings.

After one of their fellow-soldiers had brought a lever they prised off a lid. 'Rifles, sir! Winchesters.'

The officer nodded and turned to the man whom his sergeant had brought before him. 'You in charge of this business?'

'I'm the ferryman, sir.'

'Who owns these guns?'

The man shook his head. 'I didn't know they were guns, sir. Believe me. I assumed it was ordinary commercial trade.'

'I didn't ask for excuses,' the officer growled. 'I asked who they belong to.'

The man shook his head again. 'Don't know, sir. I just ply the ferry.'

'Is it your ferry?'

'Yes, sir.'

'Then unless you work for nothing you must have been paid. So who paid the toll-charge for these damn wagons to be brought across?'

The ferryman pointed across the river. 'Some guy in Matamoros, sir. Don't know his name. Think he was an agent for the owner.'

The officer made a dismissive gesture with his hand. 'Get back to your tub before I slam you in the stockade for gun-running. Sergeant, see that these guns are taken to the arsenal.'

He strolled along the front, noted the bales. 'Who's in charge of this cotton?'

A bespectacled old gent in a suit came forward. 'I am, *m'sieur*. It belongs to me.'

The officer gave him a scathing look. 'Damn Frenchies. Why don't you keep your noses out of our affairs?'

'I have been here many years, *m'sieur*. I think I have earned the respect of the community.'

'This cotton,' the officer went on,

'looks like it's headed for the ferry.'

'Yes, *m'sieur*.'

'You got government papers?'

'No, *m'sieur*.'

'Then it stays where it is. There is a prohibition on the exportation of cotton except by authorized agents of the government.'

'But, *m'sieur* — '

'Any back talk,' the army man bellowed, 'and the cotton will be impounded while you will be slammed in the stockade for contravening Federal regulations.'

From his distant vantage point the sheriff had heard and seen enough. Unnoticed he continued along the river and worked his way up between the shacks into town. All along the main street stood clusters of Union soldiers.

He pushed through the law office door to see the agitated face of Al, one of his deputies. 'There's Union men all over town, boss.'

The sheriff dropped into the chair behind his desk and let out an exasperated sigh. He raised a hand and jabbed a finger at his eyes. 'You see these things here, Al? They're called eyes.'

'What we gonna do, boss?'

'Kick 'em out of course.'

'But there's too many, boss.'

The lawman looked at his deputy and shook his head. After a moment he said, 'Things are sure gonna change around here.'

10

The door of the law office banged open and the Union officer that McGann had seen at the riverfront was standing before him, two soldiers on either side.

The man took off his gauntlets and slapped the dust from them. 'Major Grayson, United States Cavalry. Are you the duly elected peace officer of the town?'

'Yes, sir.'

'I'm here to officially inform you that the Union army under the command of General Banks has taken repossession of Fort Brown.'

Fort Brown had been built in the 1800s to protect the Rio Grande border area. The town of Brownsville had grown up beside it in a two-way relationship. It serviced the fort while the fort protected the town in its trade across the river. Years ago, when the fort had been abandoned by the military it had been given to the town.

'You are probably aware that the French have seized Mexico,' the man continued. 'Under the Monroe doctrine the United States is opposed to that act on principle. But more important there is the possibility that the Frenchies might now join forces with the Confederacy. Thus the Federal government is in the process of occupying all those parts of Texas that border Mexico. Our own unit is now based in Fort Brown with a detachment here in Brownsville. Plus the river will be permanently patrolled.'

'It's a big river.'

'Nevertheless, we can cope. Any traffic that does not submit to our command will be blown out of the water.' He walked forward and dropped his backside on the desk and some relaxation entered his voice. 'Now, let me make it clear at the outset that we do not intend to cause any inconvenience to the resident population. After all, we are all Americans, yes? Our purpose is not to subjugate. As far as you're concerned that means as law officer that you will remain in your post and it will be your responsibility to maintain civil order. To that end you and I will liase on all appropriate matters. Have you got any problem with that, Sheriff?'

'No, sir.'

The major put out his hand. 'In that case let us hope we have a fraughtless relationship.'

After he had shaken the proffered hand, the sheriff pondered on the matter, then said, 'You mean we are on equal footing?'

'In a sense.'

'So I can speak openly — officer to officer?'

'Of course.'

'In that case, you must allow Monsieur Duval to ship out his cotton.' He was thinking as much about his cut of the transaction as he was about the upholding of regulations.

'You've heard about that matter at the waterfront?'

'A law officer has to know what's going on. The point is, we got news a month back that all restrictions on the export of cotton have been revoked.'

'You got evidence of that?'

The sheriff rummaged through his drawer to find a document which he handed to the soldier.

The man nodded after he had perused it and handed it back. 'It seems in some matters you are more up to date than I.' He closed his eyes and rubbed his hand across a tired-looking face. 'We've been in the field since April. Very well, no embargo on cotton.' Then he smiled wearily. 'You see, we can work together, Sheriff.'

He looked across at the stove. 'Does Southern hospitality extend to a cup of coffee?'

'My apologies. Al, fix a drink for the major.'

'Strictly speaking,' the army man mused while the deputy set about his task, 'with us walking in on you unexpectedly like this, I suppose 'hospitality' is not quite the right word to use in the circumstances.'

'It'll do,' the sheriff said.

There was silence for the length of time that it took to get coffee mugs into all their hands, then the sheriff asked, 'What happened to the Confederate forces hereabouts?'

'Yes, we noticed there was a detachment of the gentlemen in grey. But the representatives of your armed forces, quite sensibly, retired without resistance.'

The sheriff absorbed the information. 'And how many men involved in this occupation?'

The army man smiled. 'Come, come. I have said that you and I are to work closely together — but not that close. That's classified information. But I'll tell you one thing, we have sufficient strength to carry out our orders. Namely, patrol the river around Brownsville and make sure no more contraband crosses the Rio Grande. And to be on the lookout for spies. And, of course, to counter the menace of any invasion the Frenchies might make.'

★ ★ ★

Father Enrico noticed that a couple of altar candles had hardly any wicks remaining. He carried them to the vestry. He took a knife from a drawer and gouged out the vestiges of wax. He used a rag to bring a shine back to the metal of the holders. From a large cardboard box he took two new candles. As he worked them into place his stomach rumbled to remind him it was mid-morning and time for a bite — and his regular relaxation activity.

Back in the body of the church he restored the candlesticks to their former positions.

Wiping his hands on the rag, he took stock of the interior and noted how the flowers hung colourless and lifeless from their vases around the walls. One more task before his snack and regular appointment. He genuflected before the altar and began the circuit of the building, collecting the dead plants.

As he approached the front from the side aisle, the main door opened and two rifle barrels nosed through. He stopped alongside the door and quizzically monitored the proceedings. Eventually the weapons were followed by two uniformed soldiers, slowly inching their way in.

'What's the meaning of this?' he boomed.

The two startled men whirled round to show him a pair of grimy but young, wispy-chinned faces, neither of which had yet felt a razor blade.

'We're looking for Confederates,' one said toughly.

'There are no soldiers here,' the priest said. 'Now take those wretched weapons out of here. Firearms have no place in the House of God.'

'Not until we've checked it out for

Rebs,' the young spokesman said defiantly.

The priest hurled the mass of dead flowers at the speaker and with two strong hands grabbed the barrel of the nearest soldier's rifle. He yanked it forward pulling its holder with it, while simultaneously ramming his foot against the lower shin of the young man. Thus the soldier had forward impetus but not mobility and sprawled on his knees as a consequence.

In a fast and neatly executed manoeuvre, the priest hefted the weapon into a firing position and swung it in the direction of the remaining soldier. 'Mebbe you didn't hear me, young man. I said no weapons in the House of God. Now drop that thing and kick it over here.'

Priest and soldier stood facing each other — gun to gun.

A less than benign smile came to the priest's lips as he stepped clear of the fallen man. 'I'll tell you, kid, you want to act stupid, you're in the right place for a funeral. Now do as you're bid.'

The soldier contemplated the threatening muzzle for a few moments further. The coolness of the man in the robe and the expertise with which he had dispensed with his comrade suggested the man knew how to fire the thing in his grip. Slowly the soldier complied and booted the weapon across the flagstones.

'You ain't always been a priest,' he said as his gun rattled to a standstill at the feet of his challenger.

'That's right, kid. I ain't always been a priest — like you ain't always been a soldier.' He motioned for the downed man to rise. 'Now, the pair of you, take off your hats and show due respect in the House of God. Then you can tell me what you are doing here.'

'The town has fallen to the Union, Father,' the spokesman said, a quiet deference now marking his speech.

'When?'

'The early hours this morning.'

'Any casualties?'

119

'No. There was no resistance.'

The priest absorbed the information, then: 'Bad news and good news. At least I thank the Lord for the good news that no one was harmed.' He nodded around the church. 'Well, as you can see, here are no soldiers here, Confederate or otherwise. So, unless you want to pray or make your confession in the confessional over there, to which you are quite welcome, I think you should leave.'

The soldiers eyed each other, then nodded.

'At long last,' the priest said, 'some sense.' He shucked the rounds from each gun in turn and returned them to their owners. Then he accompanied the young men outside and watched them descend the steps.

'Jesus,' he muttered when they were out of earshot. From his high vantage point he could see specks of blue — all over town.

11

Shortly, the priest was walking through the town, nodding his head at deferential greetings along the way. Occasionally he would stop and have brief exchanges as townsfolk apprised him of the morning's developments.

Eventually he reached the Dirty Dollar Saloon and pushed through the batwings. Regulars nodded a casual greeting. Non-regulars looked surprised when his sandalled foot slapped onto the foot-rail and he leant on the bar, gazing around like some deprived drover just in off a cattle drive and looking for some action. When he turned round, the bartender had already poured his usual shot of whiskey.

No hasty disposals down the throat for the Lord's representative on that part of His earth known as Brownsville.

The man nodded an acknowledgement and walked across the room, his careful gait and the determined focus of his eyes illustrating his intent on not spilling any of the amber fluid. The drink was supplied gratis and as usual he would make it last all session.

Only when he had taken his usual place at the card table did he allow himself the indulgence of savouring the taste by the merest moistening of his lips. He exchanged muted greetings with Sheriff McGann and the others in the game, then took some coins from his robe and placed them on the table. Winnings went into the poor-box while any losses came out of his own pocket. His stipend was a pittance but that was no drawback: he was a good player.

Folks were used to him and never questioned why he came, supposing that it was his way of mixing with ordinary folk. If that was a reason it was a bonus. The reality was he enjoyed a drink and a game of cards.

As throughout the town, the conversation around the table was about the Union takeover of the area. He joined in the game but not the talk.

'Miguel's getting it around town you're quite some hero,' the sheriff said after a while, without taking his eyes from his newly-dealt hand. 'Spinning this yarn how you bested a couple of Union soldiers. Disarmed them and booted them out the church.'

'Miguel is a good man fresh from the seminary but he tends to exaggerate.'

'Well whatever you did, you certainly impressed him.'

'Fact is, something has to be done, you do it.'

Eventually the game finished and the players drifted away leaving the sheriff and priest.

'And what do you think of today's developments?' the lawman asked.

'We are a long way from the theatre of war. The fact that our soldiers withdrew without military action suggests there will be no fighting here. So the most we can expect is inconvenience.'

Inconvenience was not the word the sheriff would have used to describe the loss of his take from river traffic but he made no comment. He pointed to the priest's nearly empty glass. 'Another one, Father?'

'No thanks, Bill. One a day suits me fine.'

The sheriff rose and before leaving to replenish his own glass, pushed his tobacco pouch across the table. 'There's the makings. Help yourself to a smoke if you've a mind.'

When he returned from the bar his companion was puffing on an ably constructed cigarette. He took a drink and eyed the man for a while before saying: 'You know, I've never seen you as being in the normal run of a priest. Don't know what it is. Cut from a different cloth, so to speak.' He chuckled at the figure of speech he had coined. Then, he said, 'Come on, we've known each other for some time. I don't know anything about you. What is it that accounts for your being different?'

'Different? Every priest is different. Each person on God's earth has different circumstances, has a different background.'

The sheriff rejected the reply with a shake of his head. 'Come on, Father, you know what I mean.'

Enrico sighed, resigned that he would have to tell his tale to keep the peace. 'I suppose I am marked by spending as much time in the lay world than that of the liturgy. Where do I start? I was raised on my folks' spread up in North West Texas. Not much of a place but we got by. My given name is Henry but I was Hank in those days.'

'How does Enrico come in?'

'The locals down here tagged me Enrico when I first hit town and it's stuck. Guess it's Mex for Henry. Anyways, there were four of us brothers. Naturally Pa wanted us to learn how to handle things so we could take over when the time came. The other three went along with that but I was restless. I knew there was something else I wanted to do. Then I got the calling as some describe it, and knew what it was I wanted to do. Ma was happy that I had an ambition but Pa — a rugged man of the practical world with no use for books — just couldn't understand. Anyway I left and took up training for the priesthood. Eventually, for my probationary period I got sent to a small place out on the frontier. Little nowhere place called Dry Bluff. At first I was full of all the pep of a wide-eyed youngster. But in time a frustration set in. It was real wild country and I could see evil all around me but there was nothing I could do about it. With little law to say things different, the ordinary folk were being oppressed by big boys who had taken over the town. The old story. Parishioners would come to you with their troubles and they all centred on these lawless critters. You feel so helpless when the best you can come up with is 'I will pray for you, my son.'

'It came to crux one day when the hardcases were roughing up one of the townsfolk who wouldn't kowtow with protection money. Wanted to make an example of him for the rest of the community so they were deliberately playing the whole thing out on Main Street for all to see. There was gunplay and the poor fellow was killed. I'd just got to the scene to try to help him but I was too late. In the heat of the moment I grabbed his gun and before I knew it I had put down three of them, including the two ringleaders. I don't know what came over me.'

'These guys must have been regular gun-merchants. How could a priest pull off such a stunt?'

'Back on the ranch we learned most of what there is to know about horses, cattle, roping — and guns. It was all part of the requirements for our life. Anyways, there was a couple of hardcases left standing and they just lit out of town.'

The priest smiled at the look of incredulity that had appeared on his companion's face, then he continued. 'When the story reached the church authorities it was decided my action had not been appropriate for a man of the cloth and that I should find occupation elsewhere. For some unknown reason they gave no credence to my defence that I had eradicated evil from the town. Church history down the ages is littered with schisms. This was another one.

'So I was stuck without a job. There's no money in the ministry but at least you've got a roof over your head. I didn't know what to do and was thinking of returning to my folks' place. Meantimes, the tale had got around the territory and offers started coming in from other towns, offering me hard cash to clean up their towns. I had time on my hands, no money, so I became what in the business is known as a 'troubleshooter'.'

The sheriff nodded. 'Yeah, I've heard the term.'

'The way I saw it, it was simply another way of doing God's work. A more positive way. As they say, actions speak louder than words.'

The sheriff mulled over the story, then asked, 'And how come you returned to being a more orthodox priest?'

'A fellow changes. I was a hot-headed youngster in those days. I got older, things happened and I returned to the fold.'

'Any regrets taking to the cloth again?'

Enrico finished his drink and rose. 'It's a mite quieter.'

Outside they walked straight into a blue-clad officer with the insignia of captain.

'Ha, Monsignor the infamous priest,' he said in the patrician tones of New England. 'This is convenient. Saves me a walk up to that church of yours.'

'What can I do for you, my son?'

'My men tell me that this morning

you were guilty of non-cooperation with the occupying forces.'

'Since when has non-cooperation attracted guilt?'

'As and from three a.m. this morning you, like everybody else, are subject to military law.'

'As and from the day you were born and until the day you die — and after — you are subject to God's Law.'

'Never mind that tattle. I am second-in-command to Major Grayson, who has been appointed administrator of the town, and I am not a man to be crossed. So remember the name: Newland. Captain Newland. Mark it well because, should you contravene emergency regulations again, I will see to it that that piece of cloth will be no protection. Good day, *Father*.'

The two men watched the officer turn and march regimental-style down the boardwalk.

The sheriff smiled. 'What was that you were saying about things being quieter?'

130

12

Lieutenant Stringer kept his horse at a canter down the gentle grade that led into Brownsville. Hitting the street he pulled his animal to walk. He'd heard that the Union had moved in and was reassured to see blue uniforms liberally about the place. He dismounted at a junction and looked around, figuring that the road west, hemmed in on both sides by false fronts, constituted Main Street. While still taking in the scene, he watered his horse at a trough. Then, walking the animal, he continued down the slope towards the river.

At the bottom he maintained his vigil, noted the ferry off-loading on the other side. He swatted a fly from his face. A northerner, he wasn't used to the heat, sticky humid from the river; nor the damn insects it spawned.

Back in town he walked along the

rutted road, past stores and saloons, still weighing the place up. He could hear as much Spanish as English spoken. During the days of Mexican rule, Brownsville and its sister city of Matamoros had been one. One of the legacies of those times was that now both languages were spoken equally on either side of the river.

Eventually he spotted the law office. He tethered his horse at the rail and barged into the building without knocking. There were two badge-packers, one seated at a rickety table, the other sprawled on a dilapidated chaiselongue, horsehair straggling out of cracks, an ancient cast-off from some rich planter's drawing room. They looked up, startled at his unannounced entrance.

'What the hell . . . ?' the reclining one blustered, shaken from his reverie.

Without speaking Stringer appraised them both, then crossed to the desk. 'Which of you two is the head lawman here?'

'Neither,' the one at the desk said. 'The boss has finished his morning shift. Usually in the Dirty Dollar at this time.'

'No matter, you'll do.'

By this time the one on the chaise longue had uprighted himself. 'Around here, mister, civilized folk allow even humble deputies the courtesy of knocking before they come in.'

The visitor ignored the comment. 'I need some information.'

The two young men exchanged glances across the room, both still concerned with the man's attitude. 'Well, as for myself,' the one at the desk said, 'I pride myself on minding my own business.'

Stringer's hand shot across the table and grabbed the front of his shirt, pulling him close. 'Listen, you southern trash, I said I need some information.'

The other deputy went for his gun but before he could draw it, the soldier had whirled to one side and drawn his own. 'Just give me trouble if you want a pistol-whipping and time in the guard-house for the duration. I'm a Union officer on official business. Do you understand the situation, Reb?'

A deferential 'Yes, sir,' came in unison from both.

The lieutenant sheathed his gun and took out his documents: first his identification paper, then the picture of Murdoch. 'Have you seen this feller come into town? Last seen he was with a woman driving a wagon.'

The two lawmen studied the likeness and shook their heads.

'Well, remember his features. He's a wanted spy booked for a firing squad. Any Rebs who aid and abet will get the same punishment. That includes a lawman who looks the other way. So, keep a lookout. I'll be back.'

At the door he added, 'I'm under-cover so don't tell anyone other than your sheriff about me.' He patted his gun. 'Anybody finds out, I'll know who told 'em.' And the door banged behind him.

Outside on the boardwalk, a trooper was leaning against a stanchion.

'Excuse me, soldier,' Stringer said. 'Which way to Fort Brown?'

The soldier noted the military authority in the tone and looked him over. 'A pleasure to hear a northern voice for a change. Half a mile on, sir.'

'Thanks.'

He untethered his horse and, needing to stretch his legs and acquaint himself with the town's geography, he walked for a spell before mounting up.

Shortly the fort hove into view, above it the Union flag hung limp in the breezeless air. He wheeled his horse to one side to allow a detail of soldiers to march past and then he dropped out of the saddle.

A guard challenged him at the gate. He showed the man his papers. 'Need to see your CO,' he explained.

The soldier looked the documents over and returned them. 'Why no uniform, sir?'

'Special business.'

The man nodded. 'Well, the general's a busy man, sir. He may not give you time.'

'You can see how far I've travelled. I think he'll do me the courtesy of seeing me.'

The guard turned to another in his detail. 'Corporal, take the lieutenant to General Banks.'

Stringer tied his horse to a rail just inside the fort and crossed the parade ground. Several buildings were rubble and a detail of shirt-sleeved squaddies were rebuilding a perimeter wall. Although the departing Confederates had given little military opposition, they'd tried to blow up much of Fort Brown as they sounded retreat.

At one of the few undamaged buildings, he was shown up the steps, across the porch and into the relative coolness of the interior.

'Who shall I say, sir?'

'Lieutenant John Stringer, 13th US Infantry, based at Alton, Illinois.'

General Banks did give him time and

the visitor was escorted in to explain his mission. When he finished he passed the officer the photograph. 'I would like copies of this likeness distributed around town, sir. If you have paper and pen I will suggest suitable wording.'

The general looked over the picture. 'There's a photographer's parlour on Main Street. He should be able to supply the service. I'll detail a man to arrange for it.'

'Thank you, sir.'

'What do you think this renegade's intentions are?'

'The last I heard he's heading this way. So figure he'd be aiming to get to Mexico.'

The general tapped the picture. 'I already have a permanent detail at the ferry together with units along the river. Once my men have this, your man will not find his objective of crossing the river an easy task. Meantimes, you wish to be quartered here I presume.'

'No, sir. I need to be watching the ferry till your men have the picture then

I want to keep an eye on traffic coming into town.' He patted his clothing. 'Less conspicuous out of uniform. What's the law situation in town, sir?'

'It's under military law but I've allowed the local sheriff to stay in post to handle civilian matters.'

'I've already run into his deputies. Southerners. Begging your pardon, sir, but is it wise to leave such responsibility with Confederates?'

The other nodded. 'Expediency, lieutenant. The arrangement will help to keep the locals happy — but, of course, the civil lawman is ultimately responsible to me.' He looked at the clock ticking loudly on the wall. 'Well, lieutenant, anything else we can do to aid you in your mission, let my adjutant know. Now, if you'll excuse me.'

'Of course, sir. And thank you for your time.'

He saluted and left the room.

★ ★ ★

'Had a visit from an army critter while you were gone, Sheriff,' Al said as his boss entered the office. 'Said he was a Union man working undercover. Showed us a picture of the man he was after.'

'You recognize the fellow in the picture?'

'No.'

'He was quick with his temper,' the other added, 'and with his gun.'

'He pulled a gun?'

'Sure did. He made a grab at Al and before I could do anything, he pulled his iron on me — rattlesnake quick.'

'What happened?'

'Showed us the picture, told us to look out for him. Said it would be a serious offence to help the guy.'

'Damn Yankees are acting like they own the town,' the sheriff observed. He looked at the clock. 'Stage is due.' Time for him to take stock of new arrivals to town. 'Look after things while I'll take a mosey up the hill.'

13

It was two days on.

The brake of the coach squealed as the driver heaved it against the wheel to bring the stagecoach to a standstill. For a moment the thing rocked on its thorough-braces. The driver and his sidekick dropped down. 'Brownsville, folks. End of the line.'

The vehicle tipped to one side as one by one its passengers stepped to the ground. The two-man crew set to work passing down the dust-covered baggage.

'How does one cross the river?' Lisbeth asked the man who handed her their cases.

'Ferry, miss. Take yourself down the road a spell, turn left, you can't miss it.'

'Thank you.' She slipped some coins into the man's hand and took Caldor's arm. They made their way along the rutted track, turned as instructed and looked down the slope to the river. They could see the ferry making its way towards Matamoros. 'There it is,' she whispered. 'The river, Mexico and safety.'

They walked down to the first of the stores and dropped their baggage under the awning on the boardwalk. 'We'll have to find out what the schedule is and see if there is another crossing today,' she said. 'So you stay here in the shade, darling, while I make enquiries.'

For a while he watched her descent along the track. Needing to stretch his limbs after the cramped conditions of the coach, he rose and worked his arms; then stepped forward to lean on the rail and watch the passing traffic. His observation was casual and he didn't realize that he in turn was being watched — but more intensely — by somebody else.

Following his routine of watching arrivals Sheriff McGann had noted the couple from the moment they had stepped down from the stage. The lawman waited for a fruit-wagon to pass then he crossed the street. At the other side he leant against the wall of the store near to the newcomer and took out the makings.

He had just fired his cigarette when a soldier came round the corner from the stage terminus. His orders were to check incomers, but the stage had been late and he had been relieving himself when the vehicle had come in. He had some catching up to do.

Seeing the baggage he approached Murdoch. 'Can I see your papers, old timer?'

Murdoch straightened and patted his pockets. 'I'm afraid I have no papers, young man.' They had been stopped by several Federal patrols during the journey and had a cover story. Thus, he was not overly disconcerted by the soldier's interest, particularly figuring the placid demeanour of the soldier indicated he had no idea whom he was addressing.

'In that case,' the soldier said sharply, giving him no chance to supply their well-honed cover story, 'you will accompany me down a block to HQ for questioning.'

Murdoch stiffened. Now *that* was bad news.

However the sheriff, shielded by Murdoch, drew his own gun and touched it to the elderly man's back. 'Don't move,' he whispered. Out loud he spoke authoritatively to the advancing soldier. 'This is nothing to do with you, soldier. Back off.'

'The hell it isn't,' the trooper retorted. 'I'm taking this man for questioning.'

The sheriff grabbed Murdoch's shoulder and moved him around so that the soldier could see the gun he had stuck in the man's back. 'See this? It's called a gun, laddie. This man was under arrest minutes before you came on the scene.'

Murdoch was non-plussed but quietly went along with things.

'What the hell you talking of?' the soldier snapped.

'You ask Major Grayson. I'm responsible for civil law — not the army. Those are your major's own orders.'

'Baloney. We question who we please. I'm taking him into custody until he's cleared.'

The sheriff raised a staying hand. 'Your major wants the cooperation of the townsfolk. He's told me himself. You interfere with a civilian officer in the course of his duty and you'll have the whole town against you. When your major's got a civilian riot on his hands and has to face General Banks, you tell him you started it — by taking a man out of legal civilian custody, despite the advice given to you by a duly elected law officer. A law officer who has the support of your CO.' He motioned to the growing crowd observing the scene. 'In front of witnesses too.'

'What's he wanted for?' the soldier asked, his tone laden with suspicion.

'He's on a charge of larceny and

theft. Now if you know what's good for you you'll do your duty and go back to your commander and tell him what's happened. Then, if this man is wanted on military matters, he can be found under lock and key in the jail yonder. What happens after that will be subject to discussion between *me* and your superior officer. Simple as that.'

'You bet your bottom dollar I'll tell my superior officer.'

'Now move,' the sheriff snarled at Murdoch. 'And get your thieving ass over to the jail.' He leant towards the storeowner who had now joined the audience. 'Look after those bags, Jed,' he whispered out of the corner of his mouth.

The two men moved out with the soldier in tow. He followed them down the grade into Main Street, finally watching them enter the law office.

'Keep your eye on the bluebelly outside,' the sheriff said to his deputy when the door was closed. 'Tell me if he goes.'

'I'm grateful you got me out of the man's clutches,' Murdoch said, 'but what's this all about?'

McGann sheathed his gun and dropped his rump on the desk. 'This may look like a God-forsaken hole at the end of the universe, my friend, but we got some principles. Union up north chase a Confederate agent down here — well, some folks might stand by him.'

'I'm at a loss to see what this has to do with me, Sheriff.'

'Down here we've been a bit slow in putting our cards on the table,' McGann went on. 'But we're Rebs too and we ain't about to see such a fellow fall back into Union hands.'

Then came a shout from outside: 'You ain't heard the end of this.'

'The trooper's going, boss,' the deputy observed.

'Good,' the sheriff said. 'But figure he'll be back soon with some authority.' He joined his deputy at the window, saying to his 'prisoner', 'Now this guy I was talking about — the one you know nothing of — if he was in town he'd have to keep his head down.'

'I still don't know what's going on.'

McGann smiled at the vain attempt at subterfuge. 'I'm sure you don't. Anyway, I should be able to fix you up at my sister Doña's place. She's got a hotel. It caters for Mexes so it won't be the first place they'll look.'

'Why are you helping me, a stranger?'

'Could be I'm just drumming up trade for my sister's business.' Checking there were still no uniforms, he moved from the window. 'OK, come on. We'll leave by the back just in case.'

* * *

Meanwhile, Lisbeth was experiencing her own shocks. Her first shock came minutes after leaving her husband when she passed the telegraph office. There was a picture of Caldor pinned to the noticeboard. Described as a Confederate agent, wanted dead or alive. It was a serious offence to harbour, aid or abet.

The one saving grace was that the likeness portrayed him as short-haired and close-shaven.

Her heart pounding, she passed on, not wishing to cause attention by studying it, and hurried down to the quay. The ferry was returning but it was of no consequence to her now. There was a detail of Union soldiers scrutinizing everyone and their activities. A Union flag hung in front of the building nearest the river, clearly marking a permanent base. Worse, the dreaded poster was fixed to a stanchion on the landing platform. And another on the wall of the soldiers' quarters. It was clear Caldor would not be able to board without close examination and interrogation. While his changed appearance had been sufficient thus far to pass casual observation, he would not survive any serious inquiry.

When she returned back up the hill she found the sheriff waiting by her baggage.

'Have you seen a gentleman here?'

He touched his hat. 'Don't worry, ma'am. He's booked into a back room in the Hotel Casa Blanca — The White House. He's quite safe there, it's run by my sister Doña. Come, I'll help you with the baggage.'

He took her via out-of-the-way alleys and they entered the hotel by the back door.

When they got to the allocated room Caldor was lying exhausted on the bed.

'Just keep out sight and you should be all right,' the sheriff said and, with no further elaboration, he bade them goodbye.

'Why should he be helping us?' Lisbeth asked when Caldor had explained events.

'Figure he's anti-Union as I am fast becoming. Only puzzlement is, how did he know who I was?'

'Because your picture is all over town.' Lisbeth relayed her own findings. 'There is nothing for it,' she concluded. 'We will have to stay until we can formulate some other course of action.

And, as the sheriff advised, you must stay in the room. Let's hope the sheriff is as discreet as his actions indicate.'

She sat on the bed and took his hand. 'And we will continue the subterfuge that you are old and infirm.'

'Huh,' he grunted, closing his eyes. 'That will not be a difficult role to act.'

★　★　★

Captain Newland bust into the law office trailing the young soldier. Sheriff McGann was alone at his desk, filling in a form.

'Right, where is he?' the captain demanded.

'If you're on about the petty thief I arrested earlier, sir, I'm afraid he's made a break.' He tapped his pencil on the paper before him. 'I'm writing out the report now. Embarrassing business. I can't tell you how embarrassing.'

The captain marched briskly in back and checked the empty cell. 'What the hell happened?'

'I was out of the office at the time. Wily old buzzard had a Derringer stashed away. Pulled it on my deputy and vamoosed. Oldest trick in the book. Young kid, got a lot to learn. I tell you, sir, the codger wouldn't have pulled a half-assed stunt like that on me.'

The officer slapped his gloves irritatedly against his palm. 'Damned incompetence.'

'Yeah. Fact is, the youngster hasn't been my deputy for long. Another bodge like this one and he won't be deputy much longer. Anyways, what did you want the feller for?'

'It's the major's orders every new-comer is checked. The corporal here tells me the man had no papers so he needed looking into.'

'Well, we're on the lookout for him. We'll let you know if we catch him again.'

'You'd better,' the officer snapped and stormed out of the building.

'Yeah,' the sheriff muttered under his breath. 'Al's a real bonehead. Think I'll suggest he joins the army.'

He screwed the paper into a ball and tossed it in the trash basket. He crossed over to the chaise longue, lay down and smiled.

14

'Is there anything I can do for you before I go?' Lisbeth asked.

'I'm fine, honey,' Caldor said from the bed. 'You take as long as you like.'

It was the next day and she had expressed a desire to go to church. He asked no questions, made no comment. He knew she was religious in a way that he was not. For her part she felt the need to thank God for safe deliverance in their journey so far, and to pray for safe-keeping in the final stage.

With a tall bell-tower the church was a substantial edifice in the Spanish style, a reminder of Brownsville's former status as a Mexican province. Indeed, with half the congregation whispering reverentially in Spanish as they milled around the entrance, Lisbeth felt she was already in a foreign country, as she had done since the moment they had come to town.

She crossed herself at the door. The sunlight filtering through the stained glass windows showed the assembly to be the usual mixture of poor and well-to-do. In choosing a pew she took care to avoid a blue-clad soldier. Was he strict in his religion or had he been sent to monitor the locals? Even though she managed to find a seat some distance from him, his presence still made her uneasy.

The gathering was quiet until the liturgy began. She felt comfort in the familiar Latin intoned by the priest at the altar. She closed her eyes and felt a measure of relaxation, rare for her in these times. But the feeling was short-lived. Strangely, she began to sense that the familiarity went beyond the words.

It was the *voice*.

She opened her eyes. The kneeling priest still had his back to the congregation. Eventually he rose, revealing that he was a man of stature.

Even though the robes masked his physique it was evident he was solidly built.

He turned — and lights of recognition exploded in her head.

The rest of the service passed in a haze and, before she knew, it was over and she was alone in her seat. Not daring to look round, she heard the priest bid farewell to the last of the worshippers at the door; then his sandalled feet behind her coming up the aisle. The footsteps stopped. She looked up.

The long pause expressed his incredulity. 'Lisbeth?'

'Hank.'

He dropped beside her and took her hand. 'I can't believe it. After all these years.'

'I can't believe it either.'

'What are you doing here in Brownsville of all places?'

She let the question pass. 'Hank, I married again.'

The euphoria left his face and he was

silent for a moment. 'Married? But we never divorced.'

'I know. Divorce is not open to us. But I do have another man. And we have lived as man and wife for some years.'

Again he was silent as things sunk in. Then his face brightened. 'How's Cathy? And why isn't she with you? She must be turning into a beautiful young lady now. Lisbeth, I've missed you both.'

She looked around. 'Is there somewhere we can talk?'

'There's the vestry.'

He took her arm and led her across the interior.

'You haven't changed,' he said as he opened the vestry door.

'Where's Cathy? And how is she?' he continued when they were seated opposite each other at a table.

She leant across and took his hand. 'I've got bad news, Hank.' She cleared her throat. 'She passed away.'

For a moment his face was frozen.

Then he breathed the word 'God' and his eyes closed with moisture squeezing out from their edges. Eventually he could manage to ask, 'How? When?'

'Some time back,' she whispered, her voice trembling and her eyes filling with tears as she relived the experience. 'There was some military action near our home. The Confederates were on the run and the Union army were sweeping through the territory. In their advance they were clearing the area of habitation and they set alight to the place deliberately.'

She explained how Caldor had gone to help a fallen soldier and had been bludgeoned into unconsciousness.

'It was all so confusing,' she went on. 'In the general mêlée, I got knocked down by a rider and I too fell unconscious. When I came to, the place was ablaze. I screamed at the soldiers but they wouldn't do anything to help. And I couldn't get back in — it was an inferno. Hank, I just couldn't get back in to her.'

He put his arms round her. 'It wasn't your fault, Lisbeth.'

'Yes it was. You see, there was an underground store. When the trouble started I put her in it. So once the fire got a grip she wouldn't have had a chance.'

They remained silent except for the sounds of their shared grief.

Then she said, 'Everything was burned. The house, the furniture, the clothing. The only thing I had to remind me of her was her doll. You remember the doll she had when she was very young?'

'Yes. It had woollen ringlets.'

'That's the one. She had clung to it over the years and it was still her constant companion. Some comfort for her in the troubled times we were all going through. Anyway, in the confusion she had dropped it outside. Next day, after the dreadful events, I came across it. Hank, it was all I had left of her. I took it with me to the army headquarters. I managed to get through

158

to the captain. I asked him, why had he killed my little Cathy? Didn't even say he was sorry. 'Regrettable' was the word he used. Just said, 'Regrettable, but these things happen in war'.'

A blankness took over her expression. 'Hank, I can hear him saying it now. 'These things happen in war'.'

She touched her forehead. 'To my dying day his features will stay burned in here. A hard man. Face and voice like granite. No remorse showing in either. Gave orders for me to be taken away. 'Sergeant, remove this female from camp' — those were his bleak words — and he simply carried on with his paperwork.'

'Who'd given the order to fire the place?'

'He had. Said they had to destroy anything that could be useful to the enemy.'

He let go of her hands and pulled his chair round the table. He sat beside her and locked her in an embrace, smoothing her hair repeatedly. 'Dear Lisbeth, what you must have gone through . . . '

She nestled against him. Eventually the hands clutching him relaxed. 'I have to go, Hank,' she whispered. 'Caldor will be worried.'

'Caldor.' He ruminated on the sound. 'So that's his name.' Then: 'Listen, I must see you again. There are so many things I want to know.'

'Yes, me too. But it will have to be soon. I don't know how long we are going to be in Brownsville.'

That prompted other questions in his head — starting with what were they doing in Brownsville? — but such questions paled into insignificance compared with the devastation wrought by the news of his daughter's death. 'Yes,' he said. 'I must see you again. But not now. I've got to adjust to . . . '

Finally, his voice more composed, he said, 'What about after the service this evening? Could you make that?'

'Of course.'

He escorted her to the door and watched her cross the forecourt and enter the main street. When she finally disappeared from view he clanged the door shut, walked down the aisle and dropped on his knees before the altar.

15

Back in the vestry he took a bottle of communion wine, uncorked it and took a long swig. He had met Lisbeth during his trouble-shooting days. At first it had been idyllic. His activities brought in good money. They took out a mortgage on a little house in the leafy part of town. He didn't think things could feel any better. But he learned they could get even better, when Cathy was born.

The only blemish on their paradise was Lisbeth's not liking his job. He never explained the exact nature of his work. All she knew was that he would be called away to help people. Nevertheless, it was unavoidable that over time snippets would filter back. Occasionally men died under his gun. He didn't intend it that way but it happened. He never told her of such eventualities but she guessed.

With time and the realization of what he did, she began to worry about his safe return from operations. And about the possibility of miscreants seeking revenge. She began to ask, couldn't he get another job?

His occupation became a serpent in their Eden. She misread his dismissal of her fears as a rejection of her feelings, a coolness towards her. In turn her feelings began to cool towards him. His fame — or notoriety — had spread wide and he had signed to a town-taming exercise up in Arizona. By that time rows between them had become regular and just before he left for the Arizona job they had had a particularly emotional exchange. She took the opportunity of his absence to leave with Cathy. On his return they had been long gone. He searched for them but during his extended absence their trail had gone cold. And it was a big country.

After a long period on the bottle, he reconciled himself to events, deciding it was time to begin again. He returned to the ministry, losing himself in its liturgies and self-sacrifice. It was some kind of surrogate, an attempt to recapture something solid. Moreover, he knew he had been at fault and the cloth provided a way to do penance for his mistakes.

And now, in Brownsville, fate had decreed that their paths should cross again.

Alone with his thoughts in the locked vestry, the wine flowed as much as his tears. Come evening, Miguel ringing the bell reminded him of his commitments and he refrained from finishing the third bottle. He hoped that washing his face would be enough to cover the signs of emotion, and he unlocked the door. As he walked towards the altar, the awareness of his responsibilities caused him to wonder if the two and half bottles swilling around inside him would impede him in his duties.

★ ★ ★

However, conducting the service had the effect of sobering him up so that when the couple met later in the vestry as agreed there was little sign of his indulgence.

They exchanged stories — but his subsequent life had been uneventful so he had little to tell.

She explained how she had eventually met Caldor, a doctor; how in time they had fallen in love. They had set up home and lived comfortably in Tennessee.

'It seems to be my lot to fall for men of conviction,' she said. 'Caldor was never involved in politics but, a characteristic he shares with you, he is a man of principle. If he hadn't gone out to help that soldier . . . '

She explained how he had been taken prisoner and transported to Alton. She described how he had been framed, branded a spy and their subsequent journey south. Her mention of Brownsville prompted her to conclude by asking him, 'And why did you come so far south?'

'Much more mundane. I simply needed to get away from places with sad memories.' Now composed and able to see things in a broader perspective he smiled and shook his head. 'This is what is called irony. Here's me, one-time man of action now twiddling my thumbs in a priest's robe. The last thing I remember of you was dressed in an apron in a cottage with roses round the doorway.'

'My dear Hank, there were no roses round the door.'

'You know what I mean. And now you're having adventures that could have come straight out of a dime novel.'

She reciprocated the smile. 'Fate plays weird tricks.'

'And what are your plans now?'

'To get away from the 'adventures' and trouble — find a place of safety in Mexico.'

'Will I ever see you again?'

She clutched his hand. 'I think it's better that we don't meet again, Hank.'

He nodded. There was much in his heart but it was best left unsaid.

16

Lieutenant Stringer clumped into the White House Hotel. The desk clerk, known to all as Jimbo, straightened his armbands and appraised the visitor. 'Can I help you, sir?'

'I want to have a look at your signing-in book.'

'Do you want a room, sir?'

Stringer leant wearily on the counter. 'Listen you dead-and-alive schmuck, if you don't show me the book I'll come round and fetch it.'

The clerk's hand went under the counter without him taking his eyes off the man and brought the book into view. The army man grabbed it and flicked through till he found the current page. 'How many rooms you got?'

'Seven, sir.'

'All occupied?'

'Yes, sir.'

The lieutenant ran his finger down the page. 'According to this, there's nobody in Number Five.'

The clerk looked quizzically at the entries. 'That is funny, sir. For some reason they haven't signed in.'

'They? Two of them?'

'Yes, sir, a man and a woman.'

'What are their names?'

The clerk was beginning to look apprehensive at the grilling. 'I really think you should speak to the Señora Proprietress. I'm not sure I should disclose — '

Stringer's hand was across the counter and around the man's throat before he could finish. 'I said, what are their names?'

'Mr and Miss Chatterton.'

'Chatterton? That sounds Anglo.'

'Yes, sir. They are the only Anglos in residence at the moment.'

'That's strange. This place looks as though it's for Mexes. This couple, they new in town?'

'Came in a couple of days ago.'

169

'They come in by wagon?'

'By stage as far as I know, sir.'

Stringer closed the book. 'Number Five, eh? Are they upstairs now?'

'I think they're out. At least I saw the lady leave some half hour ago.'

The army man crossed the reception area and dropped into a chair. He got out the makings and built himself a cigarette. The smoke was wafting up towards the chandelier when there came a shout from the landing. 'Jimbo, where's the big broom?' It was the proprietress at the top of the stairs.

'In the broom cupboard, ma'am.'

'No, it's not. I've just looked.'

'Sorry, ma'am. I remembered — I used it in the kitchen earlier.'

'Well, bring it here.'

'Yes, ma'am.'

Stringer watched the man disappear into the back, remerge with the broom, and mount the stairs. 'Don't like the look of that man below,' the clerk whispered to his lady boss when out of earshot. 'Asking about that couple in

Number Five. Looks as though he means trouble.'

'Who is he?'

'Don't know but he has a mean manner about him.' He explored his neck with his fingers. 'The weasel grabbed me by the throat. It's still sore.'

She took the broom and placed it in the cupboard. 'A hardcase, eh? Well, my brother might want to know about this. For some reason it was he who brought them here. Besides, they're a nice couple and I wouldn't like any harm to come to them. I'll slip out and notify my brother. See what he opines.'

Minutes later she was in the law office relating the situation to the sheriff.

'Jimbo wasn't sure whether they're both out,' she concluded, 'but the old man's not well and rarely leaves so I figure his wife's out by herself.'

The sheriff nodded. 'This guy's a northerner you say? I guess I know who it is. Snooping bastard.' He raised his eyebrows in embarrassment. 'Excuse my blaspheming, Doña. Tell you what. I'll come over and sit on that rocker outside. That way when she or they come back I'll be on hand if'n there's any trouble.'

Some twenty minutes later Lisbeth returned and the sheriff allowed a few seconds to pass before following her into the hotel.

Inside she nodded an acknowledgement to the clerk and ascended the stairs, without giving a glance to the man who had left his chair and started to follow her. Outside the door of her room she opened her bag to extract the key.

'I'll take that, ma'am,' Stringer said.

'Oh no you don't. Raise you hands.'

He half-turned and saw the sheriff with drawn gun.

'Get your nose out of this, Reb.'

But before he could stop him, the sheriff had nipped forward and taken his gun from its holster and stepped back to a safe distance. 'Attempted robbery in broad daylight, dead to rights.' He motioned with his gun. 'Hands up and get down those stairs.'

'What the hell you doing?'

'Taking you to the law office to lay formal charges.'

'You bozo, I'm an officer of the United States Army on official business.'

'Yeah, official enough not to be in uniform. Now move.'

'The town's under martial law,' Stringer chuntered as he made his way down stairs. 'Military law takes precedence over civil.'

'Civil law's still operative. Ask your precious major.'

Minutes later Stringer was behind bars. 'You're going to regret this,' he snarled waving his paper.

'I'll look at whatever you've got when you've cooled down,' the sheriff said. He feigned a grimace and rubbed his stomach. 'Meantimes I'm going to fetch my lunch. This fracas is interfering with my eating habits and that plays the bee-Jesus with my ulcer.'

He moved very quickly across the road, calling for his sister as he burst through the hotel door. 'Doña, *rápido*. Get me a tortilla or bread wrapped in paper so it looks like my lunch. That's the excuse I've made to get out. I'm heading back to the office and am going to keep that fellow in the jail for a quarter-hour. Use that time to hide the old feller someplace and get another old man — doesn't matter who — into the couple's room.'

The moment he returned to his office, his prisoner resumed his ranting at the lawman. 'Your deputies know who I am. They've seen my papers. Here have a look for yourself.'

The sheriff ignored him and positioned himself at his desk with his back to his prisoner so that the man couldn't see the hastily prepared packet he had brought. He opened it and ripped off a chunk of bread. He munched very slowly, then closed up the packet and crossed to the stove. Taking his time, he went outside to dispense with the dregs from the coffee pot and get a refill of water.

After ten minutes he looked back at his prisoner. 'You want some coffee?'

'I want to get out of here.' The man thrust his hand through the bars and waved his paper.

The sheriff checked the clock. A fair amount of time had passed. 'Very well, let's see what you've got.'

He took another sip of coffee and strolled leisurely back to the cell. He took the paper without looking at it. 'Now, I came across you attempting to rob a young lady. What have you got to say about that?'

'I wasn't trying to rob her. I was after her key. I needed to see inside the room.'

'And why would you want to do that?'

'Look at that damn paper. Certifies that I'm an officer of the United States Army.'

The sheriff read the words. 'This could be anybody. Just because you're in possession of it, doesn't mean it refers to you.'

'Yeah, in the same way that you having that badge on your chest doesn't mean you're a sheriff. Listen, check with General Banks or Major Grayson.'

The sheriff saw a chance for further delay. 'But this paper says you're based at Alton, Illinois. Unless the major and his superior know you personally they're just inferring your identification from this piece of paper in the same way that you want me to. Why did you need to search the lady's room?'

'It's possible she's harbouring a wanted Confederate agent. That's why I'm here. Your deputies must have told you. I checked with them when I first came to town.'

The sheriff shook his head. 'No, they didn't tell me. Neither of 'em are the best at remembering.' He looked at the clock and satisfied himself enough time has passed. 'OK, I'll give you the benefit of the doubt.'

He opened the cell door and held out

the paper. Stringer grabbed it and brushed past him. 'Major Grayson's going to hear how you impeded a Union officer in pursuance of his duty. We'll see how your precious civil law stands then.'

Minutes later he was knocking at the door of Room Number Five in the hotel.

Lisbeth opened it and he pushed her aside to step brusquely into the room. Only to see, stretched out on a bed, a wizened figure bearing no resemblance to anybody he had ever seen.

17

The man everybody knew as Swampy leaned on the tiller. It was a long flat-bottomed boat carrying timber down the Rio Grande.

Having grown up in the Mississippi swamps — hence his tag — he'd lived on water and had been a river-man as long as he could remember. His skills and knowledge of river traffic had enabled him to earn a dollar on the boats of the Grande. The trouble was he couldn't keep a dollar. His penchant for gambling and drink saw to that.

It had been a long trip and he was looking forward to relaxing in the familiar saloons of Brownsville. Only hours away, the rest of the journey was routine so, out of sight of the others, he had begun his celebrations early; his anticipation taking the form of opening the bottle hidden in his large jacket.

It was a fine day. The only sounds were the occasional creaking of the hull and the dull wash of waves against the sides.

He was alone at the helm. There'd been a slight slippage of cargo and the skipper was aft with the rest of the crew adjusting ropes. He looked back and noted they were fully occupied in their task. Then, when the captain disappeared once more from view, he drew the bottle from his pocket and took another long draught. He'd been at the helm for some time, long enough to have emptied half the bottle.

He saw some soldiers bivouacking near the bank. Blue-uniformed troopers. During their trip they'd heard of the takeover of Brownsville so he was not surprised to see Union men. He smiled and waved. Some waved back. Damn Union bastards, he thought and let the false smile slip from his face after they had passed.

He took another drink and steered the boat around a gentle bend. Ahead the river was relatively straight — the home stretch! Not long now. He pondered on the evening to come. The bright lights. And, with his paypacket padded out with bonuses, there would be more drink, some cards and maybe even a woman.

His dreaming carried on this way until there was an almighty crunch. The whole boat juddered and began to slew round as men tumbled to the deck. Suddenly the craft was alive from prow to stern with skipper and crew — heavy-footing round the decks, scrambling over the cargo, some looking at him, others looking over the side, all yelling.

It was obvious what had happened: they'd hit a sandbar. With increasing drainage upstream the river was lower year by year. As an experienced river-man he knew the existing and potential dangers, which is why he had been put at the helm. But hooch has a certain way of neutralizing the benefits of experience.

Captain Vanhal stormed up the deck. 'What the hell you doing, you pissant?'

He grabbed Swampy by the collar and pulled him close. 'Damn booze,' he snarled when the potent fumes hit his nostrils. He pushed the man away. 'You know I don't allow liquor aboard!' He took the bottle from the man's pocket and slung it as far as he could into the river. He ordered another man to take the tiller, then joined the others in trying to free the vessel using barge-poles.

Some Union soldiers jeered at them from the bank.

In ten minutes they were free but there was a problem. Water was seeping in through the planking near the prow. That was too much for the skipper and he ordered a rowboat over the side. He manhandled Swampy into it and with a couple of crew rowing, ferried him to the riverside. When the bottom hit shallow water he heaved the drunken man out.

He took out his wallet and extracted

half a dozen bills, throwing them in the water.

'There's your money,' he said. 'And no bonuses. I gave you your last chance, you drunken *dummkopf*. You won't work for me again and I'll see to it that no other skipper in Brownsville takes you on.'

Still bleary-eyed Swampy splashed around in the shallows, clumsily trying to retrieve the pieces of paper. Finally he looked up to see the skipper still shaking his fist as the oarsmen rowed hard to catch up with the cargo-boat.

Still standing in the water Swampy looked down at the sodden money in his hand. Half a river-man's pay consisted of bonuses so what he was staring at was a pittance. In fast depreciating Confederate money too.

He stepped up onto the bank and sat down. He shucked off his boots and emptied the water out of them. Now he needed a drink more than ever. And it would be well after nightfall when he made it to Brownsville. If he was lucky.

18

Lieutenant Stringer watched the freight being loaded onto the ferry. Finally it came for the passengers to board and he joined the sergeant checking them. Recognizing him, the sergeant saluted and continued with his task. The lieutenant scrutinized each face but there was nobody remotely resembling Murdoch amongst them.

When the ramp was hoisted up he watched the vessel push off, then pointed to the picture on the sergeant's desk. 'You sure this feller nor any critter like him has crossed the river from here?'

'Sure as hell, sir. Nobody boards without a close inspection.'

'What about before you had the poster?'

'My own lieutenant asked the same question, sir. We can't recall having seen any guy like him.' He cast his eye around his men who nodded in agreement. 'We've kept an eagle eye ever since we were put on this detail.' He waved the papers in his hand. 'See, we already had a couple of Confederates to look out for from the start so we've missed nothing. I think we would have remembered the guy.'

'Carry on,' the lieutenant said, saluting, then walked up the slope towards the town. There was always the chance that Murdoch had got across the river just before the occupation. But the varmint would have had to have been further ahead than he figured. Or maybe his quarry had made the crossing from another point. However, the river was lined with sentries day and night watching for any activity so that chance was remote.

He strolled along the main street and into a saloon. There were several drinkers dotted around. Looked like locals and the usual river-scum. At the back a gaggle of oldsters were playing cards for cents. They must have been at it a spell, most of them manifesting a degree of noisy inebriation.

He bought a beer and took it to a table. One way or another he had to find Murdoch and silence him. And it had become personal; he couldn't brook anybody standing up to him. He had looked forward to being in charge of the firing squad that would have put paid to the pissant once and for all. Then the wily critter had escaped from under his very nose. Yes, sir, this thing was personal.

He was still pondering on his next move when the card game broke up. The fellows carried on drinking for a while until one by one they made their staggered exits. Stringer paid them little mind, grateful that he didn't have to suffer their raucous noise any more — until one of them caught his attention. Looked familiar. Then it struck him. It was the old fellow who had been in the hotel room with the woman.

Out of instinct he decided to follow the guy. He had no plans and the fellow intrigued him. He was further intrigued when, once outside, the guy moved in a direction opposite to the hotel.

The army man had no trouble keeping on his tail as the old bozo was only capable of a slow, irregular stagger. Eventually the man turned up an alley. At the end he opened a door and virtually fell into the building. Interesting, Stringer mused: the fellow had not knocked the door, a strong indication that he lived there.

When he got to the now closed door, he leant against it and listened. A raised female voice was complaining at the guy's state.

He knocked. The door was opened by a woman, funereal-looking in a black, bombazine dress, about the same age as the old codger — who was now sprawled out in a chair behind her, breathing noisily with his eyes closed.

'Excuse me, ma'am. That gentleman, he live here?'

'Who wants to know?'

Stringer took out his identification and turned it to the light coming from the room.

'No trouble, ma'am. Just a routine enquiry.'

The woman grimaced. Incapable of reading, she assumed the paper was official and said, 'I have to admit, sir, that the gentleman is my husband.' She turned back to look at the immobile figure and sniffed haughtily. 'But at times he is no gentleman.'

'And he lives here?'

'Of course he does.' Then her tone changed. 'What's it all about? He drinks too much but he's never been in trouble before.'

'As I said, ma'am, just routine. Sorry to have troubled you.' With that he touched his hat and returned down the alley.

So if the fellow lived *here*, what had he been doing in the woman's hotel room the other day? There was an obvious answer and judging by the harridan who had answered the door he could understand why the guy might seek solace elsewhere.

On the other hand . . .

He headed back to the saloon to think things through.

★ ★ ★

Swampy Morgan stared into his empty glass. Another few nights like this and he'd be out of jack. Damn boat bosses. Stuck together like flies on manure. News would already have spread about the afternoon's episode. A river hand could be forgiven for a mistake or two. But not the cardinal sin of grounding a boat while hitting the bottle. The skipper had meant it. Swampy wouldn't be taken on by any boss working the river out of Brownsville. They operated like one of those fancy New Orleans gentleman's clubs. Once the word was passed on between them, you were permanently blacked. Jeez, he couldn't even earn cents from sweeping out saloons. He had been caught too many times helping himself to the merchandise.

He upended the glass out of habit and absent-mindedly sensed the last drops touch his lips while he thought. There was no point in trekking out to the coast. Damn Yankee blockade had made sure there was no work available there. No point in trying to get back to his home state of Mississippi — that would be looking for trouble, trekking through a war zone. Of course, up-river there was Laredo. But that was a hundred miles or more, and he would have nothing to live on while he made the journey.

Then there was Matamoros. That was simply a matter of getting over the river. He fought to control his bleary eyes while he counted the remnants of his cash. Yeah, if he didn't drink any more he had enough for the ferry ticket. Trouble was he didn't speak Spanish. Plus, although Brownsville and Matamoros were in two different countries and separated by the river, they acted as one town and the boat bosses operated out of both. He guessed by now he was probably blacked over there too. Besides, the Mexes had their own troubles across the water, what with the Frenchies taking over and all. Could be out of the frying pan into the fire.

He contemplated his meagre grub-stake. Hell, he was stuck in some trap. Because the war was pushing up prices daily, even when you got money you had to spend it right away. And you were in a double bind if paid in the Confederate currency that nobody wanted. Even your own kind turned their noses up at it.

He looked up and saw a big fellow enter and walk to the bar. The first thing that struck him was the northern sounds of the man's speech. Huh, another damn foreigner. Since he'd returned from up-river, he had noted the preponderance of blue about town. On the way downstream they'd heard about the Federal occupation of Brownsville — but it was a jolt to witness it.

But the more important thing was the second thing he noticed about the fellow: the thick wad of bills the guy pulled out of his pocket to pay for his drink, solid Union money too.

★ ★ ★

Stringer had his own matters to ruminate over. He seemed to be at the end of the trail. But there was one thing nagging at his brain. Something small, but odd: the fact that the drunk that he saw tonight had earlier been ensconced in the hotel room. No rhyme or reason to it. Unless . . .

With no leads to go on, he had time to check it out. But he wasn't going to go blundering in there again. Might attract the attention of that damn sheriff. Not that he couldn't handle the sheriff. He could have a word with the major — or General Banks if need be — and invoke martial law to put the pipsqueak lawman in his place. But, if there was an innocent explanation to the matter, he could look a jerk. Also he knew the major wanted to maintain relationships with the civilians and he couldn't afford to get on the wrong side of him.

On the other hand, if he could get to the upstairs of the hotel without the clerk or proprietress seeing him he could conduct his investigation without attracting undue attention. That would be his course of action.

He quaffed his drink and headed down the street.

He turned up the alley running alongside the hotel. After he had waited a few moments for his eyes to adjust to the darkness he could see there was nothing but clapboard and a window too high to reach. He moved round the back to find that that provided no ready access either. Around the corner at the far side he was in luck. Steps mounted the side of the building leading to a door at the first floor.

He contemplated the prospect for a few seconds.

But that was a few seconds too many. He felt an arm whip round his throat pulling his head back and tremendous pain in his stomach. Before he could utter a sound a hand was over his mouth and he began to crumple.

Swampy Morgan finished off the kill by slitting the man's throat with the large blade carried by all river-men. The kind of life he led ensured that, despite drink, he could pull his faculties together when necessary and his eager eyes had noted exactly which pocket the large bill-fold was in. Consequently the matter was over in seconds and he was working his way through the darkness at the back. Two blocks on, he turned up an alley to emerge into the street. Checking he had caught nobody's attention he headed for his flop-house cot down on the waterfront.

19

The sheriff looked down at the body. It was a mess. The stomach was gutted and blood from the slashed throat stained the ground around the head.

'Oh boy, this is going to mean trouble.'

He looked up and down the alley. It was early morning so, thankfully, there were no sightseers.

'Al, get over to the funeral parlour and tell them to expect a client and to make due preparations. And, Jed, see if there are any soldiers about and bring one here.'

Some five minutes later a white-faced corporal was by his side. 'You know that fellow, son?' the sheriff asked.

'No, sir.'

'Well, it's my understanding he's a Union officer working undercover. Inform your major. I've arranged for the remains to be taken to the town undertaker a block down the street but I'll delay movement of the body until one of your officers has had a look at the scene in an official capacity. Then I'll be in my office if the major wants me.'

'Yes, sir.'

As the corporal departed the sheriff walked the length of the alley studying the ground, but found nothing untoward.

* * *

General Banks sat, elbows on desk, his fingers steepled. On hearing the news he'd called both Major Grayson and the sheriff to Fort Brown. They were in his office standing before him.

He looked at the blood-stained paper before him. It was Stringer's identification document. 'This man was an army officer,' he said. 'He was on an authorized army mission. And I figure he was killed because he was onto somebody. That makes it a military matter.'

'If you'll allow me, sir,' the sheriff said, 'it's got all the hallmarks of a riverside killing. The river workers carry knives and know how to use them, sir. I've seen this kind of thing before. If you'll allow me an opinion, sir, it looks like a straightforward robbery. The guy's bill-fold was gone.'

'You don't have to kill your victim if it's just robbery, sheriff. Even in a God-forsaken place like Brownsville there's some logic to people's actions.'

'There's a lot of folk — we call them river-scum — who don't hold life very high, sir. Live in squalid quarters like river rats all along the waterfront. It's not unknown for them to knock each other off. Brawls and such. Only difference is, usually the body disappears down the river.'

'Anything else?'

'As you know, neither I nor your own men could find anything at the scene to point a finger.'

'Well, I can point a finger,' the general snapped. 'And I'm cancelling our arrangement. You've shown you're incapable of maintaining law and order. I'm installing my own provost marshal to handle civilian matters.' He looked at the clock on the wall. 'Vacate your office by noon. That'll be all.'

The general waited for the lawman to leave. 'Now, let's hear no more of what the former sheriff thinks. Jesus, what do we expect him to say? He's Confederate, for God's sake. He's bound to say it has nothing to do with the conflict between the states. He'll say anything to minimize military boots walking over his precious little bailwick.'

He drew the wanted poster closer. 'No, it's this Reb agent, Murdoch. That's the guy Stringer had chased down here. The Reb spy is here. What's happened is: Stringer came across this Murdoch who somehow got the better of him and killed him. The point is where is he now? I've ordered all sentries to report back about movements out of town last night. There have been none. So that means the Reb bastard is still here somewhere. And when we've nailed him, let's hear no talk about sending him back to Alton. I'll have him up against a wall and shot — here in Fort Brown.'

'Anything you say, sir.'

'Right, major. The town is under your jurisdiction. I want the whole place cordoned off — on the three landward sides and all along the river front. Completely sealed. Then, starting at one end, you systematically search every building in the goddamn place. If you need any more men, let my second-in-command know. He'll let you have whatever he can spare. Understand?'

'Yes, sir.'

* * *

Lisbeth stepped out of the hotel. The distant church bells reminded her it was Sunday. Every day she walked down to the quay to see if there was any relaxation in the military detail there. But as soon as she stepped outside she knew something was different. There were more people on the street than was usual for any day — never mind Sunday — and there was a worrying sense of urgency in their gait.

'Excuse me,' she said, catching the arm of a woman scurrying past. 'What's going on?'

'Haven't you heard? The military have sealed the town off and they're searching every building.'

Lisbeth looked along the main drag and could see a rank of soldiers elbow to elbow, spanning the street at one end. Behind them masses of other military were going in and out of buildings. A distant figure in white gloves, Captain Newland, was barking out orders. She spun on her heel and returned immediately to the hotel room to relay the news of the search to her husband.

'It's time for us to face facts, Liz,' he

said. 'If the town's sealed off they're going to get me this time.'

'We don't know they're looking for you.'

'As always, dearest, your optimism is displacing reality. Of course, they're looking for me. Listen, all that remains now is for us to separate so you are not caught with me.'

'As long as you are not in their hands, there's still hope. And even if you do get caught, there's still hope. You've already proved that. Now get ready. We're leaving.'

'Where to?'

'We'll find somewhere. There are lots of people about for us to get mixed in with if needs be. And the search parties are still several blocks away.'

He eased himself off the bed.

'We'll leave everything here,' she added. 'So if the staff see us leaving it doesn't look like we're moving out permanently.'

Outside they stepped unhurriedly along the boardwalk.

'That's it,' she said suddenly, as the church bells came to the end of their chimes. 'The church! We'll mix in with the congregation. At least, it'll give us a breathing space.'

Further on they managed to mingle with the crowds advancing on the church. As the worshippers bunched up at the narrow door Lisbeth leaned across to a lady beside her.

'Do you know what all the commotion back there is about?'

'Some soldier's been killed in town,' the woman whispered. Initially only a few had known of Stringer's identity and mission. But, with the killing, that few had been enough for the details to have spread like a prairie fire through the whole town. 'The story is he was after a Confederate agent,' the woman went on, 'and they're saying the agent killed him.'

Lisbeth exchanged glances with her husband as they entered the silence of the church. They settled in a pew upfront near the aisle.

Eventually Father Enrico came from the vestry and the service began. Just as he'd finished the first communal prayer he noticed the door open at the far end. He kept his eyes on the doorway as he announced the hymn and began singing. He saw two soldiers inching their way in. It was the two young men he had encountered before.

He turned to the altar, crossed himself and, still singing, began to walk down the aisle. He'd only gone a few paces when he saw Lisbeth near the front. His eyes betrayed the barest flicker of recognition but he continued down the aisle, heads turning as he did so.

'You again,' he hissed at the soldiers when he reached the door. 'What have I told you? Now get those guns out of the church.'

'But we've been ordered to — '

'*I'm* ordering you out.'

'We have to check the church.'

'Get out of God's house. Anything you have to do — you do outside.'

202

'We have to check the congregation.'

'Very well, I'll leave the door open. You can do your watching from outside. Now get out before I really lose my temper.'

The two men hesitated, then backed through the door and remained outside peering in.

'That's better,' the priest said. He resumed his singing and walked back down the aisle. Nearing the front he paused beside Lisbeth.

'Are they something to do with you?' he whispered out of the side of his mouth and holding his hymn book as though following the words. The singing of the congregation was great enough to mask the conversation.

'Yes,' Lisbeth said, her own hymn book prominently raised.

'What's happening?'

'Hank, can you help us? Give us sanctuary?'

'What's the matter?'

'The army are after Caldor.'

'Did he kill that Union officer?'

'No.'

'Then why are they turning the town inside out looking for him?'

'There's not time to explain.'

His voice boomed out once more in unison with the rest of the worshippers and he returned to the altar. He continued with the service and, while regularly looking around the congregation in the usual way, monitored Lisbeth and the soldiers.

During a pause in the liturgy he leant across to his aide Miguel, whispered something then mounted the pulpit. As the man disappeared into a side room the priest began his sermon. He spoke of the unhappiness of war. Asked his congregation to think of the men of both sides who were dying or suffering serious wounds at this time.

Eventually his aide returned with a large box which he laid beside the pulpit.

'As a token of our thoughts,' the priest continued, 'I would like each of us now to come to the altar for a blessing and to take a lighted candle. In its light the candle is a universal symbol of hope.'

He beckoned his parishioners forward, indicating with his hands the central and side aisles. As he hoped, there was a general confusion as the people rose, edging along the pews in different directions. Shortly there was a milling mass around the front. When the first people had taken a candle each, he and his aide began lighting them.

He mouthed words mechanically as his eyes flicked around the scene, checking the soldiers at the door, lighting and handing out candles, watching Lisbeth.

'Return to your seats,' he boomed, 'and meditate in silence for a while. Think of your own departed loved ones. And of the suffering of strangers. And of orphaned children. Make it your own personal moment.'

When Lisbeth approached he leant forward when he lit her candle. 'You and your husband, join the end of that group of people returning on the left,' he whispered. 'Then snuff out your candles and slip into the vestry. With God's help you might not be seen by anybody, especially by our uniformed watchdogs at the door.'

The couple waited and tagged onto the end as instructed. Seconds later they were behind the closed door of the vestry.

Lisbeth leant against a wall and closed her eyes. 'I hope we haven't been seen.'

She composed herself and looked around. There was a small door. She looked inside. It was a closet. There was a stack of varied bric-a-brac on the floor and varied vestments hanging from hooks on the wall. 'You'd be best in here for the time being,' she said.

Once Caldor was hidden away, she took up a seat at the small table and listened to the progress of the service. Eventually it finished and there was a long, relative silence. Occasionally she could hear feet and muffled voices. She itched to put her head round the door to see what was happening but managed to overcome what could prove to be a dangerous curiosity.

After what seemed an interminable period the door opened and the priest came in. 'It's all right.' he said. 'Everyone's gone. We can talk.'

She clutched his arm. 'Thank you, Hank.'

'Where's — ?' he began.

She opened the small door. 'Hank, this is my husband Caldor.'

It was the first occasion Enrico had time to appraise the man. He looked at the tired, sagging features and thinning grey hair. He wondered what Lisbeth could see in him. The man was masquerading as her father; but he looked old enough to *be* her father. His feelings about the man were mixed. Not only did he occupy Lisbeth's heart but, if it wasn't for him, Lisbeth wouldn't be in the trouble she was now in.

He wanted to dismiss the strange

interloper in their lives and take her in his arms, tell her everything would be all right. Instead, without speaking, he perfunctorily shook the man's hand.

'You should be safe here for a while,' he said, going to the door and turning the key in the lock. 'I can justifiably keep guns out. But I can't prevent men entering the House of God, even if they're wearing uniform. And if they come in force a locked door isn't going to stop them.'

He crossed to a hamper on a shelf. 'Have you eaten?'

'No,' Lisbeth said. 'Food's been the last thing on our minds.'

'Well, let's eat while we consider what to do next. This is my lunch. Simple bread and cheese but it will tide you over.' He indicated the table, then took a bottle of wine and three glasses from a cupboard. As the couple sat he placed the opened hamper between them and filled the glasses. He ripped a hunk from the bread. 'This will do me. You finish the food off.' He upended a glass and emptied it in one go. 'Right, don't make any noise. I'm going back into the church to see what we can come up with.'

After he locked the door he walked to the altar, his hands clenched. His brain was swimming. Lisbeth was back in his life. He thought of the old man, her husband. If only he wasn't in the picture, if only he hadn't survived the prison camp, or if the Federals should catch him — he and Lisbeth could start again. There had been a time when maybe he was beginning to forget, that whatever they had had was fading; but now she was back . . . he knew his love for her had never left him. Maybe he could rekindle love in her. They had known love once. And they still had the love they shared for Cathy.

Before the altar he dropped to one knee. 'Forgive me, Lord, for the thoughts I now have. Help me. Show me what to do.' He stood and breathed deeply. He paced up and down the aisle. He gazed round the silent building. A haven against the bad things that were happening outside. But for how long?

Then, back near the altar he noticed the door leading to the bell tower and he had an idea. He was walking back to the vestry when the main door opened.

It was Captain Newland.

The priest changed course and approached the newcomer.

'My men tell me you've been giving them trouble again,' the soldier barked.

'No. I told them there are to be no weapons in here. They wanted to check the congregation and I said they could do so outside at the end of the service. They've got their job to do, I've got mine. Also I told them to show respect and take their caps off. Like I'm telling you.'

The soldier grunted and removed his hat. 'Well now you're dealing with me, not a couple of rookies. *I* want to search the place.'

'Be the Lord's guest.'

The man walked the length and

breadth of the building, looking in the nooks and crannies. 'Where you from?' he asked after a first survey.

'North Texas.'

'Still — a Confederate.'

'I don't use labels like that. This is your war not mine.'

The soldier reached the vestry. He tried the door. 'What's this place?'

'That is the vestry.'

'Is it always locked?'

The priest fought to keep his composure while his mind raced. 'No.'

'Then why now?'

'It's acting as a temporary home for some orphans whose parents were killed in *your* precious war. We're looking after them in there until they can be found permanent homes.'

'Orphans? There hasn't been any fighting around Brownsville.'

'They came in with one of the parties coming south to escape from the conflict.'

'Open it.'

'I don't have the key.'

'Why not?'

'Miguel, my aide, has it.'

'And where is he?'

'I'm afraid I don't know. He's off duty at the moment. Which is just as well because the poor mites are terrified of uniforms. We don't want them disturbed.'

The soldier rammed his shoulder hard against the door but it was solidly constructed. Grimacing and eyeing the priest, he rubbed his shoulder. Then he walked towards the front and left without a word.

The priest waited a while then walked to the front door. When he saw the officer was some distance away heading for Main Street he returned to the vestry.

'You heard all that?' he said. 'The military are developing a sudden interest in the church. So I don't think we've seen the last of him. Come, I have the perfect place — the church tower.'

* * *

The priest worked fast. First he got the couple into the bell tower. It was open to the elements but there was a high wall behind which they could remain hidden.

'I'll try to stop the bell being rung while you're here,' he said. 'But it may have to be rung to allay suspicion, so rip some linen for your ears and keep it within reach.' He gave them blankets and told them to draw up the ladder.

Then he borrowed three children from parishioners whom he could trust and ensconced them in the vestry.

Just in time. The captain came heavy-footing through the main door with three troopers. One wielded a rifle and the other two carried a large log. They didn't speak as they clumped determinedly to the vestry door.

'No,' the priest the bellowed, advancing on them with raised arms. 'I've already told you I don't want the children disturbed. Is this what you call military subtlety?'

'I've told you I'm searching that room.'

As the men slung back the log in preparation for the onslaught, the priest interposed his body in between them and door and raised his hands again. 'Hold on, hold on. If it has to be, it has to be.' He took out the key and handed it to the captain. 'But please go about your work with a modicum of decorum.'

'Ha,' the soldier said. 'The mysterious key has suddenly — and miraculously — materialized. Your God can work miracles after all.' He drew his gun, keyed the lock and flung open the door.

There were two old women with their arms around three children cowering against the far wall. Straw paliasses were on the floor, blankets strewn around. He walked to the interior door and opened it. He noted the contents of the small cupboard and returned.

Back in the main body of the church he holstered his weapon. 'There's something not right about you, priest. Remember, the town is under martial law. If I find you contravening any regulations — or aiding the Confederate cause in any way — your cloth won't save you.'

He gestured to his men and they left the building.

Up in the bell-tower Lisbeth peered over the edge.

'Get down,' Caldor said in a whispered but firm tone.

'I've just got to see,' she replied, dismissing his advice with a backward gesture. And what she did see caused her to fall back against the wall, her face white. Her suspicions were confirmed.

'What's the matter, honey?' her husband asked.

'It's nothing. I'll be all right.'

20

The priest was crossing the nave on his return from delivering a meal to his high-living guests when the main door of the church opened. He'd discounted the notion of locking it for fear of creating suspicion. But there was no threat from the visitor. It was Jim Fontaine, a regular worshipper from the plantation just out of town. He walked down the aisle, hat in hand.

'What can I do for you, Jim?'

'It's my mother. The doc says that she's fading fast.'

The priest put his hand on the gnarled hand of the other. 'Jim, I'm sorry to hear that.'

'As you know,' the visitor went on, 'she's been confined to her bed for a while now. But Doc doesn't think she'll see tomorrow's sun-up — and I was hoping you'd be able to come and give her the last rites. Just in case. It'd mean a lot to her.'

'Of course.' The priest looked at his hands as he wiped them. 'Just give me a few minutes to clean myself up. You got a spare horse?'

'Transport's all took care of. I've brung the buggy.'

'I'll see you outside in a couple of minutes.'

He waited till the large door clunked, then went to the bell-tower to inform the occupants of his errand.

* * *

It was a couple of hours later. The priest stepped from the house and returned the rosary beads to his pocket. His task completed, he leant on a fence a few yards from the house and shared a smoke with his companion.

'I know you didn't get much response from Ma,' his companion said, 'but I can tell she appreciated your coming.'

'I could tell too,' the priest said. 'She's a good woman. And she has a good son.'

The other nodded. 'I'm much obliged for your coming too.' He drew on his cigarette, then grunted. 'At least, lying in her bed she hasn't had to witness the indignity of the town being overrun with damn bluebellies. Oh, sorry for the profanity, Father.'

The priest smiled. 'Sad times, bad times. No excuse necessary.'

'Union men all over the place,' the man went on. 'That would have sure broken her heart.'

The priest looked into the distance: cotton to the horizon. 'She built up the plantation with your father?'

'No. The place goes back longer than that. She was born in the house back there. When Brownsville was no more than a couple of shacks. Her parents came out from the old country and set up the place.'

'And a fine place too.'

Suddenly there was an explosion in

the distance and the priest looked around, startled. 'What was that?'

'Nothing to be concerned about, Father. Just some of my boys are clearing a field is all.'

The priest grimaced. 'For a moment, I thought the fighting was getting closer.'

'With the demand for cotton going up we're extending the growing areas. Hit rocky ground in one of the sections yesterday. Just blasting it out with explosive. I was being thoughtless. With Ma taking a turn for the worse I should have told the men not to use explosive but I forgot.'

The priest stepped on his cigarette butt and stretched. 'In the circumstances, there's another reason why you shouldn't use explosive. It's likely to attract the Union men and you'd get them all over your place too.'

'You're right.' The man put out his own cigarette. 'When you're ready, Father, I'll be getting you back.'

The priest nodded and turned to leave.

'As I said,' the fellow went on as they walked towards the buggy, 'I'm much obliged for you taking the time to come out. Anything I can do for you, let me know.'

* * *

After the service the next morning he got a broom and made a show of sweeping the outer precinct in an effort to give the appearance of normality. He stopped when he saw the sheriff walking towards the church. He wiped the sweat from his brow and leant on his broom to view the nearing lawman.

'You're too late,' he said after they had exchanged greetings. 'You've missed the service again. One of these days why don't you come a mite earlier and join in?'

'Pa was Scottish. I'm Presbyterian.'

He walked to the adobe wall and rested against it while he took out the makings.

'You got faith, haven't you?' the

priest asked, joining him.

'Oh, I've got faith in many things. I got questions too.'

'Such as?'

The sheriff finished putting his cigarette together, licked and rolled it. 'Like where have you got Murdoch and his missus tucked away?'

'I don't know what you're talking about.'

The sheriff lit his cigarette, drew hard and smiled. 'It's my understanding it ain't the right thing for a priest to lie.'

As he exhaled he studied the priest's impassive features. 'Folks say you spirited them away during the service last Sunday. Smuggled them into the vestry virtually under the noses of the soldiers.'

The priest said nothing, leant his broom against the wall and took the offered makings.

'Now they can't be there any longer,' the other continued, 'because the captain came back and gave the place the once-over. So the question is where you stashed them?'

'Folks sure seem to do a lot of talking these days.'

'Don't worry, Father. Your flock are faithful to the cause. Least, the ones who saw what you did. You know you can trust them not to tell the military. Otherwise the soldiers would have been back long since.'

'And which way do your feelings lie?'

'Do you have to ask?' He drew on his cigarette. 'The reason I mention it, I figure you might need some help. You can't do it all by yourself. The search parties are still searching the town. And that captain suspects you got something to do with it.'

'What are you telling me?'

'Priests ain't supposed to involve themselves in politics but you're a man of the world. You know the town's full of Confederate sympathizers. They ain't wearing uniforms or fighting in the field but they want to see the back of these damn Yankees as much as anyone with Southern blood running through their veins.'

He stopped talking when he noticed a rider heading their way. 'Busy day, Father. You got another visitor.' He stubbed out his cigarette. 'OK,' he said in lowered tones, 'if you won't tell me where you've got them — and I can understand why — at least give me some idea of what your plans are.'

The priest studied the eyes of his companion. 'If I can figure out what you're talking about, I'll let you know.' Then he turned to face the rider who was now reining in. It was a Negro slave from the Fontaine plantation.

The man dismounted and rubbed a handkerchief over his face. 'Excuse me, Father. Masser Fontaine sent me. Old Ma Fontaine has passed away.'

★　★　★

Captain Newland stood on the boardwalk, drumming his fingers on a stanchion. Now that the renegade was wanted for killing a Union agent it would stand him in good stead for further promotion — if he could nail him. Irritation showed in the furrowed brow and the squinted eyes with which he looked along Main Street. The situation was bugging him. The whole area was sealed off, so the wanted agent had to be in town somewhere. But where? The soldiers had tooth-combed the place. Every residence, every cupboard. And they'd turned over all the rat-infested quarters along the waterfront.

Even so, he knew in such a large town there could be some place — a space small but big enough to hold a person — that they had overlooked. Maybe somewhere too obvious that they had ignored it. But where?

He lit a cigarette and pondered. As he did so his gaze fell on the funeral parlour. What better place for a person to hide than in a container specifically constructed to take a human being! He clicked his fingers at the soldier standing near him. 'Sergeant, you were on the detail checking that side of the street.'

'Yes, sir.'

'Did you check the coffins?'

'What do you mean?'

'Did you look *inside* them?'

'Er, no, sir.'

'Come on, man.'

He crossed the street and pushed through the parlour door without knocking.

A young man was seated inside and looked up, startled by the noisy entry. 'What can I do for you, gentlemen?'

'You the proprietor?'

'No, sir. The boss is out on business.'

The captain pointed to the back of the store. 'You store your coffins in back?'

'Yes, sir.'

'Sergeant, check the coffins.' the officer ordered. The soldiers progressed through an ante-chamber with dark curtains hanging from its walls. The sergeant strode around the draped trestle table in the centre. At the far side he parted the heavy finery and entered the storeroom.

There were half a dozen boxes in two stacks. The officer watched his man remove the lids of the two top coffins. Nothing. The man rapped hard against the sides of the lower boxes and could tell by the hollow sound they were empty too.

The captain spent time examining the surface of the boxes, looking for possible air holes, then turned to the young man. 'These all you got?'

'Yes, sir.'

The captain went outside and checked the yard. Then he returned and re-examined the cramped interior. Near the wall there was a space and an absence of dust marking out a six foot long oblong area. 'There's been a coffin here recently.'

'Yes, sir. Two.'

'Two? When were they used?'

'One this morning for the guy who was killed in the robbery.'

The captain nodded. He knew of

that. Lieutenant Stringer. There had been a military funeral up at the cemetery but he had been too occupied to attend. 'And the other?'

'Old Mrs Fontaine from the plantation. Fact is, she's being buried now. That's where my boss is.'

'At the town cemetery?'

'Yes, sir.'

'Come on, sergeant. Mount up.'

* * *

Father Enrico was leading the cortege along the path. As they neared the hole the reverential silence was broken by the clop of horse-hoofs. The captain along with a sergeant and trooper noisily reined in, dismounted and tethered their horses to the fence. He strode up the path with his men in tow, and passed the procession.

'Put that coffin down,' he ordered the bearers. 'I need to examine it.'

'Have some dignity, Captain,' the priest protested.

The officer ignored him and waved a hand at the trooper. 'Use your bayonet to open the box, trooper.'

'No,' the bereaved son shouted. The priest restrained him. 'Best to allow them to do what they're fixing to do, Jim.'

The soldier drew the heavy blade from its scabbard on his belt and wedged it in the crack. He worked his way round until the lid was free enough to raise.

The captain looked in, then nodded.

'Satisfied?' Jim snarled.

'OK, put the lid back on, trooper,' the captain said. 'Sorry to have disturbed you folks.'

'Yankee savages!' Jim yelled as the soldiers returned to their horses.

★ ★ ★

After the final service, the party left the diggers to complete the filling-in of the grave. The bereaved son was still seething. 'Damn Yankees,' he said to the priest at his side. 'You wouldn't think they were Americans.'

The priest said nothing until they got to the gate. 'The explosive you use for clearing land,' he whispered, 'you got any left?'

'Is it something to do with those bastards?'

'Let's say the least you know the better.'

'Father, you can have all I've got if it means helping towards the cause.'

21

The next day Enrico entered the Dirty Dollar just as the regular card game was ending. The sheriff joined him at the bar. 'You're missing a few poker hands these days, Father.'

The priest threw his daily prescription shot back in one go.

'Drinking faster too,' the sheriff observed.

'You walking back to the office?'

'If you don't want a game of cards, yeah. The regular guys are OK, but they don't give me the challenge with a deck like you do.'

Outside they walked down a block and, reaching a deserted boardwalk, the priest leaned on the rail. He checked no one was in hearing distance and said, 'You offered help.'

'Yes.'

'Well you were right. The two

deserving cases you spoke of — I am supplying them with pastoral care.'

'Is that church language for you've got Murdoch and his wife?'

'They're in the bell-tower.'

The sheriff nodded with the hint of a smile. 'Neat.'

'And I've got to get them out,' the priest continued, 'and across the river.'

The sheriff's face became serious again. 'No easy task with Union men all along the banks.'

'That's why I need a diversion.'

'I guess you got an idea.'

'Yes. And that's where I need help. Apart from watching the river for gun-running, the Yankees are fearful of an attack from the French. You're Brownsville born and bred so I don't have to tell you that Brownsville was once Mexican territory. And it's common knowledge that Union top brass are concerned that, now the French have taken over Mexico, they may take advantage of the Union being tied up in its own war to try to expand the French empire by retaking former Mexican land.'

The sheriff smiled. 'And the Frenchies are sympathetic to the Southern cause which makes the Union uneasy about the Frogs coming over to join our side.'

'Yes, so it shouldn't be too difficult, at least for a short while, to kid the Yankees an invasion has started up river — and that'll draw the soldiers away from the town.'

The sheriff's eyes widened. 'Invasion? Boy, when you think, you think big. How you figure to do that?'

'It doesn't have to be a long distraction. Just long enough to give us time to get the couple out of hiding and on their way across the river.'

'Still a tall order.'

The priest winked. 'I've got some explosives — and long fuses.'

The sheriff pondered on the notion, then nodded. 'I see. Well, if you want to leave the arrangement of that to me I know just the place.'

'It'd be useful if there were some fires in the vicinity too. To add to the effect.'

'No problem. You know the old landing up-river? That'll be ideal.'

'Yes,' the priest said, nodding. He knew the place, full of wooden structures and derelict buildings. In former times it had been one of Brownsville's several centres for river traffic. However for as long as folks could remember the Rio Grande had been tapped with irrigation channels for hundreds of miles upstream. The uncontrolled drainage by Texans and Mexicans on both sides had taken its toll, permanently lowering the water level by many feet near the delta. With the landing left high and dry, and sandbanks exposed, the site had been long abandoned.

'There's enough dry timber there,' the sheriff concluded, 'to light up the sky from here to Houston.'

'Can such an operation be handled without casualties?'

The sheriff smiled. 'Don't you worry. The local fellers will be grateful to have a chance to put a spoke in the Yankees' wheel. This is their river — they're boatmen and shrimpers to a man. They know the dunes, marshes and levees like you know your Bible. They'll be in and gone before the Yanks know what's hit 'em.'

★ ★ ★

There was no time to lose and the operation had been arranged for that night. The hour of one o'clock was fixed as the time it was deemed a high proportion of soldiers would be asleep. A rowboat had been prepared and hidden away in marshes a half-mile downstream. A small network of trusted townsfolk had been set up to monitor the deployment of soldiers with the aim of giving the couple a clear route to the boat when the time came.

As the hour approached, the priest checked there was no one in the church, locked all the doors and mounted the bell-tower to explain the plan.

'If it's clear below,' Lisbeth said when he'd finished, 'I've got to come down to use the privy.'

'Is the pot full?' They'd been using a large covered pot for their necessaries.

'Yes.'

'Then I'll empty it as usual.'

'There's not time.'

'Very well, lower the ladder. There's no one below. The doors are locked.'

When they got to the bottom of the tower, she stopped. 'The privy was an excuse. I've something to tell you. Something I just can't keep to myself any longer.'

He grabbed her shoulders. 'Lisbeth, what is it?'

His heart rose in expectation. But fell as she answered. 'The captain who came to the vestry. He was quite agitated and talking loudly. I thought I recognized the voice. So when he came the second time with the soldiers I had a look from the tower as he left.'

'Well?'

'It's Captain Newland.'

'Yes, I believe that is his name.'

'I *know* it is his name. Hank, he's the one who gave the order to burn the house down back in Tennessee.'

'Then . . . he was responsible for Cathy's death?'

'Yes. Deliberately without warning. Otherwise Cathy would be alive today. 'These things happen in war', he said. But they don't have to. He could have given us warning.'

When he'd absorbed the information he said: 'It's been days since you recognized him. Why didn't you tell me when you first found out?'

'What would have been the point? It would only serve to lay more heartache on you, adding to the trouble we're already causing you.'

'Heartache? The emotion I feel after what you've just told me is something other than *heartache*.'

'I'm only telling you now because I can't keep it to myself any longer. It's been gnawing at me. I was going to tell Caldor but he's too ill to burden with news like that. And I had to tell someone.'

The priest turned and slammed his fist into the wall. 'Why did I choose to wear the cloth?'

There were red smears on the white adobe as he brought his fist away. 'I am not a man anymore,' he croaked, both hands grabbing and wrenching at the cloth of his habit. 'Wearing this damn thing — I have castrated myself.'

★　★　★

To start with there were half a dozen explosions in quick succession. Over the next quarter-hour the night was shattered by odd, random detonations. By then the army was being mobilized from both the fort and town.

Lisbeth and Caldor watched the scene from the safe darkness of the bell-tower. In the distance a growing patch of red bounced off the night clouds. They knew its significance and prepared to leave. Below them they could see soldiers running this way and that, shouting. Civilians emerged from houses, pulling covering over their night attire.

The couple heard a tapping below, then a voice. It was the priest. 'There are still too many soldiers about. We must wait until more have gone. So don't come down yet — but get ready. Shouldn't be long.'

★   ★   ★

General Banks stood with his officers on a rise overlooking the old docking area.

'This is weird.' he said. 'Since the initial barrage, there's been no more firing. And I don't see how shells from across the river could cause this amount of conflagration. What the hell is going on?'

He surveyed the infernos that the buildings had now become. 'And for the life of me I can't understand the military objective in shelling disused buildings. Give me your field-glasses, Major.'

He peered through the instrument into the darkness across the river. 'Can't see any activity over there at all.'

He handed the glasses back. 'Besides, whether it's the French or Mexicans, they know the geography this side of the river like they know their own. They'd know there's no military advantage to be gained striking here.'

'Could be a diversion, sir,' one of his officers said.

The general nodded. 'That's the conclusion I'm coming to, Major.' He turned to his other officers. 'Leave a detachment here. I want reinforcements at the wharf in town and other units to spread out along the river. We might be playing into their hands by bunching up like this.'

At the back, Captain Newland was musing on the situation. He approached the general and saluted. 'Excuse me, sir.'

'What is it, man?'

'It could be a diversion as you say, sir, but there's the possibility that it might not be military action.'

'What do you mean?'

'It could be the work of civilians on this side, sir. This whole business could be a diversion to cover for something in town.'

'Such as what?'

'It could be a cover to get the Confederate agent Murdoch out. I don't trust that priest for a start. I request permission to return to town to see if he is up to something. The sooner I know his where-at this moment the better I'll feel. I'd like to take some men and look for him.'

The general grunted. 'It could be a diversion for that purpose. A possibility, Captain, but a remote one. On the other hand, the scale of this thing is so large I have to cover all possibilities — even remote ones. The snag is, I need all the men I've got so if you want to make an investigation, you'll have to go alone.'

The captain saluted. 'Then with your permission, sir.'

The general returned the salute by way of acknowledgement and turned to more important matters.

★ ★ ★

When the captain got back to town there were people everywhere, standing in small groups seeking vantage points in attempts to see the fires that were lighting up the sky to the west. With most soldiers being called away now, the curfew was being rampantly ignored.

He made straight for the church. Leaving the front door wide gave him enough light to work his way down the aisle. He took a candle from the altar and lit it. He investigated the pews, looked in the vestry. He was about to leave when, back near the altar, he was intrigued to see the door to the bell-tower open. He entered and looked up. The flickering candle did not provide much illumination but it was enough for him to see there was now a ladder connecting the higher platforms. And to see that the trap door at the top was raised.

He climbed the first set of steps, then slowly began to mount the ladder. Halfway up, the guttering candle caught one of the rungs and fell. He cursed under his breath at the clatter it made hitting the boards below. Having lost any surprise he might have had, he dropped the empty candlestick and drew his gun, making the final ascent in darkness. The top platform was bathed in moonlight. And so were the blankets and plates and other evidence of residence.

'So I was right, you preaching bastard,' he muttered. For a few moments he surveyed the town from the bell-tower then descended as fast as he could.

Outside he saw a trooper, leaning on his rifle looking at the display in the night sky.

'Soldier! Have you seen anyone come out of the church?'

'There's been lots of civilians about, sir. Everywhere, coming and going. I'm sorry, sir, but with the other rankers being called away it hasn't been possible to enforce the curfew.'

'Never mind that. Have you seen the priest?'

The soldier came out with a long 'Err', then said, 'Think so, sir, now you mention it.' He pointed into the darkness. 'Someone came out of the side door down there. Looked like him.'

'Anyone with him?'

'There *was* someone with him, sir.'

'How many, man?'

'It's dark along the side there, sir, but there might have been two or three.'

'Which way did they go?'

The trooper pointed into the blackness. 'They disappeared. Reckon they went in that direction.'

'That leads to the river, doesn't it'?'

'Yes, sir.'

'OK. You stay here. And if you see the priest you arrest him and anyone who's with him. Any argument you shoot.'

'Shoot a priest?'

The captain headed into the darkness. 'Yes, soldier, I'm giving you the order to shoot. *I* take responsibility.'

22

'It's along here somewhere,' the sheriff said. A swathe of clouds had long obscured the moon, giving the party the advantage of darkness but making the task of identifying locations difficult. There was a rotting fence along the path and every now and again he would examine it. Eventually he came across a stretch of fishing net draped over stumps. 'This is it,' he said. 'The marker we arranged. Come on, this way.'

He turned at right angles and headed across the dunes towards the marshes.

'One of our fellows is going to take you across, ma'am,' he said. 'Don't worry. He knows the river like the back of his hand. Besides, the currents could be too strong for you or your husband and this guy's built like an ox. Once you get over there you're on your own but there'll be no problem for you.

There's not much of a military presence on that side — Union or otherwise.'

The group entered the water and worked their way through clinging river vegetation. After a while, a voice came out the darkness a little to their side. 'Over here, Sheriff.' The boat was so well covered with reeds that they had almost passed it without being aware. There was a gentle splash as a man stepped out of the vessel. 'Just checking it was you before I showed myself.' He discarded his own camouflage of vegetation and brought the boat more into view.

Once they'd got a grip of it, the sheriff and priest helped Murdoch to board.

'I can't thank you enough for all you've done, gentlemen,' the old man said, shaking the hand of each in turn.

Enrico took Lisbeth in his arms.

'If only things had been different,' she whispered, her lips close to his ear so that only he could hear.

'Well, they weren't. We have to be philosophic.'

'You're a good man, Hank. You didn't have to take the risk of helping Caldor.'

'Yes, I did. I can see now *he* is your way to happiness.'

'Oh, Hank.' Her voiced cracked as she spoke the words almost inaudibly.

He kissed her hair, smelt her fragrance, savoured it for one last time. 'Now you have to move,' he said firmly.

As he helped her into the boat the cloud cleared from the moon and he could see her face, the light catching the glisten of her tears.

'God speed and happiness to you both,' he said, making a brief unseen sign of the cross, and the two men heaved the vessel on its way.

They watched the boatman assert command with his oars and they headed for the shore, their job complete. But as they stepped onto dry land a shot echoed over the flatness of land and water. The new moonlight had exposed the speck of the boat battling against the current. And the same light bathed the captain with raised pistol standing behind them on the dunes.

The priest threw a glance at the river. No one had been hit.

At the same time the sheriff drew his gun and triggered it. The captain immediately swung his arm away from the direction of the boat and returned fire. The lawman spun and collapsed on the sand while the captain ran at them, firing. The priest dived to the ground and grabbed the sheriff's fallen weapon. In one flowing movement, he rolled over and fired from his prone position.

The captain pitched forward, dropping his gun.

The priest rose and keeping his weapon aimed, walked over to the soldier. He booted the fallen gun out of reach then stepped beside the man and used the other foot to turn him over.

'Why did you help him?' the soldier croaked. 'A spy. A dirty spy. You're a man of the cloth. War and politics is not the game of priests.'

'It's a long story.'

He looked down at the man — the man he hated for more than one reason. In the moonlight he could see his bullet had gone close to the heart and he smiled humourlessly. He hadn't lost his touch.

'If you don't die now, scumbag,' he said, raising the barrel so it was clear over the heart, 'I'm going to put another one of these things in you.' He knew that later he was going to feel guilt about his enjoyment in seeing the mixture of puzzlement and fear on the man's face as he said the words, deliberately slowly and clearly. Despite his vows he intended savouring the moment.

'Why? Why?' the soldier said faintly.

The priest grunted. Then: 'Like you once said — these things happen in war.'

His finger began to close on the trigger but he heard a long exhalation of breath, then saw the man's jaw slacken. He leant down, felt the man's throat and wrist. All pulse had ceased. The Lord had seen to it that he didn't need to pull the trigger again.

He stood up, feeling a satisfaction that he knew to be ungodly. Then he moved back and knelt beside the sheriff.

'Did they get clear, Father?'

'Yes.' He looked close at the man's arm. 'How is it?'

'If you'll forgive me cursing, Father, it hurts like bee-Jesus. But I think it's only a fleshie.'

'I can't see too well in this light but what I *can* make out, it's on the edge of the sleeve so you're probably right about it being a flesh wound.' He looked across at the soldier's body. 'If you'll be OK for a short spell, I'll get that bozo's remains into the river. The way the water's running he should be fish-bait in the Gulf by tomorrow. That should delay the manure from flying for a spell.'

'Then what you aiming to do?'

'First to see you back safe to town and get Doña to clean and bandage that arm. Then I figure it'll be time for me to cross the river too. Our soldier friend has probably told others of his suspicions about me harbouring Murdoch — and told them where he was going tonight. But, God willing, I should be able to get clear before the boys in blue start looking for me.'

'Mind if I come with you? I ain't got no job here anymore. And with the army clamping down on gun-running I've lost my bonuses.'

'I don't know. Can you speak Mex?'

'*Más o menos, amigo*,' he said, forcing a grin. 'Enough to get by.'

'That's good enough for me. All my time here and I never got round to learning the lingo.'

★ ★ ★

It was early the following morning and the two men walked down the ramp towards the first ferry of the day.

Between them, Enrico and Doña had bathed and patched up his companion's wound. For the crossing the ex-lawman had discarded the bloodstained jacket in favour of a clean one so as not to arouse suspicions. There was no evidence yet that the military were looking for the priest but he had dispensed with his robe.

'What you aiming to do?' the ex-sheriff asked. 'Once you're over there.'

'You know, for a good chunk of my life I knew where I was going. But the way things are panning out at the moment, even tomorrow is now too far away to make any plans.'

They stopped at the edge of the gangplank while the duty officer looked them over. 'You leaving, Sheriff?'

'You've got the title wrong, soldier,' he said. 'Now there's full martial law I ain't sheriff. So with no job, there ain't nothing to keep me here no more. Thought I'd try my luck over the water.'

The soldier looked at the priest, now in plain clothes. 'Your face looks a tad familiar.'

'Probably does, son. I'm a Brownsville resident. Like as not, you've seen me around town.'

The soldier accepted the explanation, nodded them through and they mounted the gangplank. Once aboard they walked the length of the vessel and leant on the rail without speaking, looking across the water at the land of their new life.

Minutes later they were under way.

Each lost in his own thought, they still didn't speak. Until part way across the priest leant on the good shoulder of his companion. 'Look at us, a couple of crazy fiddle-footed Texan galoots. Neither of us having any notion of what he's gonna be doing next. But whatever's round the corner, I tell you one thing — me with my Latin and you with your Spanish — I figure we got the makings of a real jim-dandy team.'

Postscript

Although history was to show that the war eventually went the Union's way, it also was to show that before the end of hostilities Brownsville was actually recaptured by the Confederates.

And in the ranks of the Volunteer Brigade that was to achieve that honour — there numbered an ex-sheriff and an ex-priest.